FITNESS KILLS

A NORA FRANKE MYSTERY

FITNESS KILLS

HELEN BARER

FIVE STAR

An imprint of Thomson Gale, a part of The Thomson Corporation

THOMSON
™
GALE

Detroit • New York • San Francisco • New Haven, Conn. • Waterville, Maine • London

THOMSON
™
GALE

LIBRARY OF CONGRESS CATALOGING-IN-PUBLICATION DATA

Barer, Helen.
    Fitness kills / Helen Barer. — 1st ed.
      p. cm.
    ISBN-13: 978-1-59414-585-8 (alk. paper)
    ISBN-10: 1-59414-585-7 (alk. paper)
    1. Food consultants—Fiction. 2. Health resorts—Fiction. 3. Baja California
(Mexico : Peninsula)—Fiction. I. Title.
PS3602.A77535F58 2007
813'.6—dc22
                                        2007005480

Published in 2007 in conjunction with Tekno Books and Ed Gorman.

Printed in the United States of America on permanent paper
10 9 8 7 6 5 4 3 2

Dedicated to Harris, for always being there for me, and to Julie, for her loving support, as well as to the members of Marijane Meaker's Ashawagh Hall Writing Workshop, for their tough love.

PROLOGUE

Saturday, early afternoon

He lay face down on the rocky slope, long legs splayed out at impossible angles, arms dangling awkwardly from their joints. His head was cocked to one side, as though he were listening to a distant conversation. From above, he looked a bit like a frog.

High on the narrow stone ledge from which he had fallen, his companion stood transfixed by the surprising speed at which both of their lives had been transformed.

Was he dead, or did he just knock himself out on the rocks? His ankle looked distorted—maybe broken. Even if, by some miracle, he came to and tried to pick his way down the knobby slope of the mountain to the safety of the spa, he'd never make it by sundown. It would be cold tonight. There would be animals roaming through the hills. And by morning, surely he'd be dead.

CHAPTER ONE

Saturday afternoon

"Tilt that pelvis, pull in those abs, now squeeeeeeeeze those buns. Keep 'em up there and lift, and lift, and lift. And five and six and seven and eight . . ."

I tried to block out everything but the tiny drill instructor's voice rising over the insistent beat pumping out of the speakers. The aerobic exercises hadn't gotten much easier to handle over the course of the two weeks I'd been working at the spa as a food consultant, and I thought everyone in the whole colorful garden of spandex could hear my gasping breaths.

I'd been desperate to run away from a dreary New York November. I needed to get some distance from my ex-lover, and (not incidentally) lose some of the thirty-odd pounds I'd gained eating my way through the breakup.

Max and I were crazy about each other; we just couldn't live together. Our lifestyles—even the hours we kept—were so different. And I could no longer handle his spoken and unspoken judgments about my weight and work.

My best friend and agent, Judith Lewin, was thrilled with the solution she'd found for me: a two-month assignment as menu consultant at Rancho de las Flores in Baja California. I was to pinch-hit for their nutritionist of many years, who was on maternity leave. My job was to bring the spa's 1960s spartan vegetarian menu into the twenty-first century. Then I was to go home and write a Rancho de las Flores cookbook. Guiding the staff through new recipes was part of the package, as was a four-times-a-week cooking demonstration class for the guests.

Judith had convinced the spa that my growing reputation as a food writer and restaurant critic would garner publicity and invite inquiries. So far, no one was complaining. Perhaps most importantly, to me at least, I'd already lost seven pounds, partly from not being able to overdose on bagels and chocolate mint chip ice cream, and partly from pushing myself through as many exercise classes as I had time for. I'd never be a passionate exerciser, but I was faithful at least.

I hoped it would be worth the personal price I was paying to be here: despite bravado in e-mails to friends and family, I was lonely. My ex-lover, Max, a chronically thin, fit, squash-playing overachiever, mocked my escape to a "fat farm"; my mother complained about my missing the family Thanksgiving orgy; and my longtime client, *MetroScene Magazine,* bemoaned my absence during the crazed preholiday season. At least I wouldn't have to worry about having a date for New Year's Eve.

"Ahem."

I opened my eyes, startled. Standing several miles above me was an elongated Giacometti sculpture. An impossibly long-limbed, long-braided blonde. Of uncertain age, but certain elegance.

"It's going to get pretty chilly in here, once the sun drops behind the mountain. Best rise before your sweat congeals." Her voice, a gravelly drawl, was softened by amusement.

"Yes, of course, I'd better get up."

Flustered, I pulled myself awkwardly to my knees and scrambled to my feet. I'd been daydreaming so long that the music had stopped and we were the only ones left in the airy, screened-in gym.

"You a new guest?" she asked, walking over to the water fountain.

I followed her.

"I work here, for the next few months at least. I'm Nora, Nora Franke."

"I'm Allison Foster Evans. From Tucson. And I guess I do know who you are now. Saw your name on the bulletin board at the lodge. We're just thrilled to have a minicelebrity here."

I wasn't sure if she was referring to my height—I was, as Max always delighted in telling me, "vertically challenged"—or the degree of my celebrity-ship. Being only an inch and a half over five feet not only made it hard to see over people's heads at the movies, and meant that I had to shorten everything I bought, it also made it difficult to appear grown-up, much less authoritative.

"I don't really think of myself as a celebrity, mini or otherwise." I couldn't help smiling.

"One never do, do one?" Allison smiled back. "I love food—subscribe to everything in sight. *Bon Appétit, Gourmet,* even, heaven help me, *Cooking Light.* I've read your stuff. You're good. I like your style."

I laughed. "I like your style, too, Allison. But I can't believe you like food that much. Not with your figure."

While I laced up my sneakers I looked sideways at Allison. Just as I thought. Just the type that made me feel as though I'd been walking around all day with a glob of mascara beneath my eyes.

"Honey lamb, I'm an absolute slave to diets," she said, slipping on the jacket to her butterscotch warm-up suit. "And I'm a spa junkie. Here one week in the fall. Mustique, in February. In the spring, maybe the Golden Door. I hear there's a real toughie in the mountains of Utah—very good for masochists. It beats throwing up after meals. You know, what those bucolics do."

"Bulimics. They're the ones who throw up. Bucolic is what

11

they wish they were."

"See? I just knew you were one smart lady!"

For some reason, Allison seemed set on charming me. It sure was working: I felt like a high school kid wanting to be accepted by the alpha girl.

Allison sighed. "Can't imagine where my buddies are," she said. "Everyone usually shows up for the warm-up class soon as they get here. Hope there are no snags in the plans this week."

"You come here with a group?" I asked. It seemed so unlikely.

"Well no, not a formal group. A few of us, a couple of men and a few other women, have always shown up the week before Thanksgiving week. By now it's a ritual."

She shrugged. "Ready to head on out?"

As I followed Allison into the chilling air, I watched her walk. So that's what they mean when they tell you to reach up out of your waist . . . stand tall . . . keep your shoulders down . . . tuck your tailbone under. It looked easy. It didn't feel easy.

"Didn't you bring a warm-up suit with you? Or sweats?" Allison scolded as I shivered and zipped up my thin windbreaker. "You must need them on the mountain hike."

"Not to worry, Mom. There's no way I'm going up a mountain. It's enough that I subject myself to a so-called meadow walk at dawn."

"By the end of next week I could get you chugging on up Mount Cuchuma. I'll bet you a 'no-no' at lunch."

"I may not be lunching this week," I said with surprising enthusiasm. "I've signed up for five days of the liquid fast. I thought I'd better try everything the ranch offers. And I could use a quick weight loss. I don't think I'm supposed to do too much vigorous exercise on the liquid stuff," I added.

Maybe I'd convince myself if no one else.

"Must be hard to hold your weight down if you're in the food business," said Allison sympathetically.

I nodded. There was no way I was going to tell this pencil-thin apparition about my moment of truth in the dressing room of the Banana Republic, when I'd broken down in tears in front of the three-way mirror.

"Who's in this group of yours?" I asked, gasping for breath as I tried to keep up with Allison's brisk pace. "Are you just spa friends or do you see each other at home?"

"Yes. Well, partly yes. There are seven or eight of us. We met here, over the years, and keep in touch by e-mail. We all take this fitness stuff pretty seriously. Can you imagine, not one showed up for class! Will I crow! They wouldn't have moseyed on up the mountain without me, I don't think." Allison cast a speculative eye at the mountain looming to the left of the path.

With some relief, I spotted my casita among a nearby cluster of stucco cottages with red-tiled roofs.

I pointed toward it. "There I am. Be it ever so humble."

I could see the steam rising from the heated water of the nearby hot tub as it hit the chilled air. "I'm wiped. Me for a hot bath."

"I'm for relaxing in my Jacuzzi with some Absolut on ice," said Allison, waving good-bye and striding uphill toward the more upscale villas.

"Look for me at dinner, won't you?" she called back to me. "I'll save you a seat at our table."

I shouted back, "Hey, thanks!" And meant it. I definitely wasn't the shy type, and the staff at the ranch was pleasant and polite; I'd never had to eat alone. But making stilted conversation with perky twenty-two-year-old fitness instructors got wearisome after a while. I'd felt more connection to Allison in twenty minutes than to any of last week's various tablemates.

As I drew nearer to the tiny porch of my casita, I was, as always, enchanted by the smells. During the heat of the day, it was like being in a warm room filled with bowls of potpourri.

Even now, eager to strip off my clammy exercise clothes and soak in a hot tub, I lingered to smell the spicy air, heavy with the almost poignantly sweet scent of honeysuckle that came from the wild tangle of vines curling over the gate to the meadow beyond. I walked toward the gate and looked across the acres of cactuslike ground cover and ice plants, enlivened with splashes of brilliant reds and yellows.

The mountains hovered beyond, almost bare of trees, ornamented instead with otherworldly outcroppings of rocks, and sliced by dark lines that I knew were hiking trails. I felt a sudden atavistic awe of the mountain. It looked malevolent. For a moment, before I went inside for my bath, I felt its power, and I shuddered.

CHAPTER TWO

Saturday, early evening

It was cold on the mountain: puffs of breath from the climber were visible by the light of the cresting moon. The harsh sounds of labored breathing mingled with the moans and whines of the wind to break the chill silence. It had been a feverish climb, a race against the setting sun, but it was imperative to see if the man lived.

There he was, spread-eagled against the rocky slope, still motionless. Even in the fast-disappearing light, the movements of small predators could be seen creeping beneath the shiny blue warm-up suit. The climber's harsh breathing slowed, and calmed. It was time to retreat. Time to leave the man to the elements and the night creatures.

I'd been lazy getting ready for dinner, soaking luxuriously in the hot bath. It had been an effort to keep from closing my eyes and sliding all the way into the water, much less to keep dry the newest copy of *MetroScene Magazine*, sent to me by the office. Amazing the tendrils of FedEx. Despite the lack of newspapers, individual telephones, and television at the ranch, packages were delivered to hyperkinetic guests on a daily basis.

As the mango-scented bubbles soothed my skin and nerves, I wondered how different my life might have been had I been more my mother's child than my father's. Had I lived more in my body than my dreams. Would my muscles ache as much

today? Instead of skipping rope and playing stickball on my
neighborhood streets, I could usually be found in a deeply
upholstered chair in the corner room of St. Agnes Library on
Amsterdam Avenue, working my way steadily through the
children's collection.

I added more hot water, and smiled as I thought of the
children's librarian, Miss Anderson, tall and blonde and stately,
an older woman (she was probably around thirty). She had
taken a quiet liking to me and encouraged me in my literary
ambitions. Yes, she had assured the nine-year-old Eleanora, it
was perfectly legitimate to want to read *A Tale of Two Cities*
instead of Judy Blume. She would write a letter to my fourth-
grade teacher. And she did! I was allowed to borrow only four
books at a time, so I had to make a weekly visit to the library.
Finally, in one of the high points of my childhood, I sat before a
committee of three librarians before they would issue me a
regular library card, thus allowing me to escape from the
children's room. I remembered Miss Anderson's pleasure as I
confirmed for the other librarians that I had indeed read all the
books they cited from the kids' section. My father was as thrilled
as I when I showed him the yellow "adult" card. My mother
was at a meeting. And today I'm well-read, overweight, and trying to overcome years of indolence.

After my bath, without turning on any of the lamps, I lit the
fire that had been carefully set out by the maid. The flames
leapt up almost at once, illuminating the charms of my room.
While it was no bigger than an ordinary motel room, it was
lifted dramatically out of the ordinary by bursts of Mexican
pinks and oranges and yellows. Local pottery sat on the stone
mantel and wooden tables, and colorful hangings warmed the
whitewashed walls.

It was a delicious treat having this lovely space to myself. I
lived alone, in a funky walk-up on Riverside Drive overlooking

the Hudson River, but had spent much of the past two years shuttling back and forth between Max's spare, elegant Upper East Side apartment and my cluttered aerie. Living in my own totally anonymous, borrowed space was giving me a welcome jolt of the unexpected. On my arrival here I'd twirled around and around, gloating. "Mine, all mine," I'd thought with glee.

My stomach growled. Time was running out. I stared at the clothes hanging on the rod against the wall. A sea of black. Thinning, if funereal. I wondered, for the zillionth time, what it would be like to just pull on clothes appropriate to the weather and occasion without obsessing about whether they'd fit or make me look heavier. I had finally settled for black corduroy jeans (with an elastic waist) and an oversized burgundy cowl-necked sweater. I felt less vulnerable than when I was letting it all hang out in sweats and a T-shirt. Big silver hoop earrings and black leather western boots finished my urban cowboy look. I fluffed up my dark wash-and-wear curls and tugged on my old standby leather jacket. Ready as I'd ever be. To meet Allison's group of friends.

No television, no radio had intruded on the almost palpable silence as I dressed. Just the noises next door.

Since my casita was in a group reserved for senior staff, or for guest speakers, it was less luxurious and closer to other units than those of paying guests. And although the adjacent cottage had been empty all the previous week and earlier in the day, tonight suddenly there were lights behind the cheery orange cotton drapes. I could hear drawers opening and closing with considerable force, and wondered briefly at my new neighbor's hurry, or temper. The lights were out by the time I left for dinner, however. And the cottage next door was again quiet and still.

Standing outside my casita in the soft twilight, I felt suddenly overcome by loneliness. Despite the fact that my days were busy and challenging, and dinner tonight promised companionship, I felt hollow. That bastard Max Weber. I was standing here by myself in the Mexican high desert and he was probably out partying. It was Saturday night. Around nine thirty in New York. Was he in bed with someone? No, too early. Where would he be? How could I find out? My cell phone didn't work here, and there were no phones in the rooms, but there was a telephone (for emergency use) on a stanchion along the path to the dining room. This was definitely an emergency.

I picked my way along the flagstone path, stumbling from time to time as I moved as quickly as I could. I'd forgotten my flashlight, but I was too impatient to go back for it. The lantern-like fixtures set alongside the walk cast soft, diffused light over the flower beds, but didn't do much to illuminate the path itself. When I found the phone, I had to peer closely to read the instructions. Fortunately I'd remembered to bring my telephone card with me.

I placed the call to Max's apartment, waiting impatiently through all the beeps and whirs of the international call. When his machine picked up, I was crushed, then furious. He was out. Son of a bitch. He was having a life without me. Instead of leaving him a message, I impulsively punched in the code he used to retrieve his calls. At least one useful thing I'd learned during the months we'd sort of lived together. Call one, his mother. Calls two and three, his sister and his mother. Call four, his best friend, Zack. Call five, bingo. Some trilly-voiced female named Diana. "See you tomorrow" indeed. Without hesitation, I erased all the messages. Who the hell was Diana?

I walked even more quickly now, concerned that I was late and hoping to get rid of some of the jealous anger I felt. Didn't matter to me who he was seeing. Sleeping with. Was she thin?

As I turned the corner around a tall saguaro cactus with raised arms that reminded me of a traffic cop, I saw the brilliantly illuminated dining room. I was so intent on my thoughts that I crashed head-on into a tiny curly-haired redhead coming from a path on the right.

"Whoosh," she said. "You sure do pack a wallop."

"I'm so sorry," I said. Then, seeing that my victim was smiling, I added, "At least I'm soft."

"That's okay. I wasn't really looking where I was going either. I was hoping I'd bump into one of my buddies, stays up your way. Missed him earlier. Anyway, I'm Cecilia Clayton. But everyone calls me CeCe."

"I'm Nora Franke."

We walked up the broad steps to the dining room.

"Oh my," cried CeCe, stopping abruptly. "You're the food lady Allison told me about! You're joining us for dinner, aren't you?"

"Yes, I am."

She looked like an eighteen-year-old ingenue, but was wearing sizable diamond stud earrings (hadn't the ranch brochure recommended "no jewelry"?) and a skinny white jersey jumpsuit. Topping the luminescent ensemble was a red fox vest, which she hugged to herself.

"You'd think I'd get used to the cold here at night," she complained. "I come often enough. 'Course, Dallas is just a minute from here. Have you met the rest of our group, Nora?"

"No, I just met Allison at this afternoon's stretch-and-tone class."

"Alan wasn't there? Big teddy bear of a fella?"

I shook my head.

"Just don't understand it. I saw him at the airport. We even chatted a minute. And I couldn't understand that either, why he was at the airport. He lives the La Jolla side of San Diego, so he always drives."

"Well, he'll probably be at dinner," I said, not really

interested. "How many in your group?"

"Eight or ten, depending. But we're going to slide another chair in, for you. We're dying to pick your brains about the menu, Nora. Get ready to defend!"

CHAPTER THREE

Saturday dinner

There was a world-class traffic jam at the dining room entrance, preventing me from having to respond. CeCe hugged Carmelita, the smiling Mexican hostess, and pulled me toward a table in the back. I smiled hello as I passed the tables occupied by the fitness staff. They looked as pleased as I that I wasn't joining them this evening.

Allison sat in regal splendor at a large round table, somewhat isolated from the other, smaller tables in the bustling dining room. She was wearing her long blonde hair in a loose chignon tonight, and she looked older and more elegant than she had this afternoon. The table faced the massive stone fireplace that dominated the room, but was just far enough away to avoid a direct blast of heat. She paused briefly in her conversation with the man seated next to her to wave us over, then continued talking with him. CeCe pulled me along and plopped me down beside her. She blew him a kiss across the table.

"This here's Nora Franke, Simon. She's the new food guru here. Nora, please meet Simon Neel."

Simon smiled blandly. I murmured a hello.

What a hunk, I thought. Movie star looks. And didn't he know it. The gray in his rugby shirt matched his eyes perfectly.

"Where's Jody?" asked CeCe. Without waiting for an answer from Simon, she turned to me and said, "Jody is Simon's wife."

"She went over to the office to find out if Alan called. He

probably just got a late start. I don't know why everyone's making such a case out of this."

What a spoiled, petulant voice, I thought with satisfaction. I didn't want to like him; he was too handsome. And he'd looked through me as if I didn't exist. I knew the type well enough: if a woman wasn't very young, very slim, and very sexy, she might as well be Minnie Mouse.

"Simon sweetie, don't be such a grump," said Allison. "I told you CeCe chatted with him at the airport, and you know Alan hates to drive over the mountain pass at night."

"So he's here somewhere."

Allison stroked Simon's arm in a calming, possessive way. I watched his cranky expression smooth out, then tighten again as a young, athletic-looking woman joined the table. Simon's wife. I tried to disguise my surprise. Jody Neel was as sexless as Simon was hot. She was slim and straight, with boring, short brown hair and soft brown eyes. Tidy-looking. Probably a few years younger than I, around thirty-three or thirty-four. Her dazzling husband was more my age.

"Dolores says Alan checked in," she said. I had to strain to hear her; she had a soft, whispery voice. Annoying. She poured some water from the pitcher on the table and gulped it down thirstily. "He's in Casita 6 . . ."

"Oh, then he must be my new neighbor," I said. "I'm Nora Franke. I'm in 5. I heard him crashing around earlier this evening, unpacking I guess. But why would he be in the staff area?"

"He's married to a former employee here," said Allison. She had subtly moved away from Simon when Jody joined the table. "Mariana's a local girl. She was assistant manager. That's how he met her. Lots of her family still works here. So Alan gets special rates."

"And special treatment," said Simon.

"You're jealous, Simon," said CeCe.

She was laughing, but no one else was. Simon looked only mildly irritated at CeCe's remark, but Jody seemed upset. She kept playing with her water glass, rubbing her fingers around and around the rim, making a squeaky sound. I was relieved when, as more people joined us, Simon touched her arm and she put her hands in her lap.

It was hard for me to focus on the introductions Allison was making—I'd begun to feel overloaded with new faces, new names, new identities. Cheeks were kissed, shoulders were hugged, gossip was exchanged. The chatter from surrounding tables swamped me.

"Nora Franke?" a voice called out. "Sounds familiar. Where you from?"

I turned to a new neighbor across the table: a tall, dramatic-looking woman with masses of long dark hair. Her manicured red fingernails clicked restlessly against the tiled tabletop.

"I'm from New York City. And you?" I asked, although I'd bet my potential royalties that I knew the answer.

She nodded. "East Side? West?"

"A walk-up on Riverside Drive. In the eighties."

"I'm crosstown from you." She snapped her fingers. "Got it. You're the food writer. I know your name, of course. I'm in PR." Her large, mascaraed green eyes inspected me closely. "I thought you'd look different."

"I think Nora looks perfect, Phoebe," said CeCe, rushing in to fill the silence. "That ruffle of black curls and deep blue eyes." She turned to me. "You must be Irish!"

I laughed. "Not unless there were Gaelic Cossacks marauding through Russia in the last century."

"I can't wait to hear all about your glamorous life," CeCe rushed on. "All those fancy restaurants . . . What's your favorite?"

"Oh, I've got lots of favorites, for lots of reasons. Aquagrill, for the most succulent oysters. Gramercy Tavern for its diabolical chocolate mousse with black-mint ice cream. Barney Greengrass in my neighborhood for yummy lox and bagels, not to mention rice pudding . . . and One if By Land Two if By Sea for sex."

Everyone except the PR lady laughed; the restaurants I named were probably not her clients.

Allison leaned forward, her elbows on the table, and fixed me with an impudent smile. "You have sex at the restaurant? On the table or floor?"

It was my turn to laugh.

"The restaurant just gets me in the mood," I explained. "Sensuous food, candlelight, low music, flowers, a fireplace . . ." I was lost for a moment in memories. That bastard.

"Whew," said Allison, waving her fingers as if they were scorched. "We'd better eat. I'll play mama."

She lifted the ladle out of the tureen that had been set beside her by a silent young waitress. "It's the color and smell of asparagus . . ." She looked questioningly at me, and I nodded.

"It's not cream-of, but it's still good, I think," I said. "You can always add salsa." I pointed to bowls of mango salsa.

Jody made a face and whispered something to Simon. I doubted it was complimentary.

"You ever get sick from a restaurant meal, Nora?" asked CeCe.

"Oh yeah, twice, from bad fish. And I've suffered through more truly terrible dinners than you can imagine. Steak with raspberry glaze. Beautifully presented curries disguising over-the-hill lamb. I never go alone . . . I need to taste as many meals as I can . . . but it's getting to the point I practically have to drag people in off the street when the time comes to review the trendy new places featuring raw food, or yet another nouvelle

Thai restaurant."

"Oh, poor baby," said Allison, laughing. "Why do you do it? Why not just review cookbooks, or teach?"

"When it works," I said slowly, thinking out loud, "it's magic. I love the alchemy of cooking. Watching creative chefs transform raw ingredients and ugly bits of animals into delectable, tempting meals is a turn-on for me." I shrugged, a little embarrassed by my poetic ramblings.

Allison stared at the platter being offered by the waitress.

"What is this?"

"Vegetarian tortillas, Señora. Whole wheat."

The waitress made the rounds of the table, as everyone helped themselves to the vegetables, brown rice, and tortillas.

"I'm going on the liquid fast for a few days, starting tomorrow. Anyone joining me?" I asked.

CeCe beamed at me. "Oh yes, I always fast for two days. A super beginning to the week."

I sighed. "My idea of fasting used to be not eating between meals." I helped myself to another serving of tortillas.

Nearly everyone at the table was scooping up as much of the elusive tortilla filling as they could. Several were calling the waitress back for additional tortillas. The conversation returned again and again to food. How would I change the menu? Was it truly fair to call it vegetarian if it included fish? Did I disguise myself when reviewing a restaurant? I answered with only half my attention; I was fascinated by the diverse personalities at the table and the tensions beneath the surface. Allison was keeping on eye on Jody, who was eyeing Allison out of the corner of her eye and hadn't uttered a word. Simon was equally silent, but restless and grim. CeCe chattered nervously. Circles within circles.

"I sure was surprised to see Alan at the airport," said CeCe suddenly. "We talked a bit 'bout a problem he was having—you know him. He was sort of talking to himself, out loud. Said he'd see me here. So . . ."

"God, I'm so sick of this fascination with Alan's whereabouts," said Simon, putting his fork down with some force. "He probably got here early, met someone he liked, and is off fucking his brains out."

Jody winced.

"Oh no, no," cried CeCe. "I just know Alan isn't fooling around here anymore."

"Or any less," said Simon.

"He promised Mariana. He told me he did," CeCe said.

"Alan talks too much, to too many people," said Allison.

"How come Mariana doesn't come here with him?" I asked.

"Sometimes she does. Occasionally she's even stayed with her family while he's been here. But now they have a baby boy—Jorge—and I guess it's easier if she stays at home."

"Easier for Alan, certainly," said Simon. He turned to Jody and spoke to her quietly. She nodded, and they both rose.

"We're skipping dessert and what passes for coffee. Maybe we'll take a walk or check out tonight's movie. 'Night."

Allison impatiently waved them off, then turned back to CeCe.

"What kind of problem did he say he had?"

CeCe shrugged. "I promised him I wouldn't talk about it. He was looking for you, probably to tell you about it."

Allison looked off into the distance. Then she gave a shrug, and said, "Well, while it's surely unlike him to miss a meal, I don't intend to call out the marines. Or his brothers-in-law."

"Mariana's family's too nosy," CeCe agreed. "Remember the fuss Emilio Cerillo made when he saw you and Alan having dinner in Almagro, Allison? He just leaped to dumb conclusions!"

Allison concentrated on her rhubarb pudding.

26

"I think I'll head on back to the casita," I said. "I have some menus to review and I'm beat."

"I just loved hearing you talk about your work, Nora," said CeCe. "To hear how passionate you feel about food, and cooking, and stuff. I don't feel passionate about anything, except my husband, Buddy. And my babies."

CeCe rummaged around in her bright red tote bag and pulled out a studio portrait of twin boys, about two years old.

"What about you, Allison?" I asked. She fascinated me. I admired her looks, and her humor. But I did have her pegged as a lily of the field, the spoiled rich wife of a CEO, on charity boards and benefit committees.

She smiled at me mischievously.

"Money. Money's my passion."

I admit it; I was taken aback. But now, after dinner, with chairs being pushed back and people from other tables coming to greet Allison and CeCe, now was not the time to pursue this.

I set off, shivering a bit in the cold air that hit me as I walked outside. Tomorrow, I promised myself, I'd stop in at the boutique. I had not been prepared for velour jumpsuits and red fox vests. Maybe I could buy something wonderful to cheer myself up. If they had large enough sizes.

I paused on the path. Suddenly I felt reluctant to leave the bustle of the dining room for my isolated retreat. There was something reassuring about the distant murmur of voices, the occasional laugh. Although why I needed reassuring . . .

"Nora? You stuck in place?"

I jumped, startled by the swiftness with which CeCe had appeared before me.

"Just moon-gazing," I answered.

"Isn't it fabulous here? It's the only place my Buddy'll let me come alone." Her voice dropped dramatically. "I've never told him there are men here."

I laughed, and after a moment, CeCe joined me.

"Oh Nora, I do love it here. I can be me. I can wake up whenever I want, strut around my gorgeous villa naked as a babe, take hour-long bubble baths. I can get endless massages and facials. I don't have to pretend to be interested in good works, or fuss about nannies and baby sitters . . . and benefits, and going to boring business dinners with Buddy. Does that sound too tacky selfish?"

"It sounds honest," I replied, knowing in my own terms just what she meant.

"You sleep real well now, Nora honey. Tomorrow's a big day. We're going to make a new beginning. Start the fast, take good care of ourselves. I just can't wait to get going. Night-night."

CeCe's soft drawl came floating back toward me as I stepped up to my patio. The dark mass of Mount Cuchuma loomed now in the deepening shadows of the night. Why did it make me feel apprehensive?

CHAPTER FOUR

Sunday morning

One of the huge logs crumbled in the lodge's oversized fireplace, waking me up. Suddenly chilled, I struggled out of the depths of the leather armchair and shoved it closer to the dying fire, then collapsed back into its shelter. With my toes, I edged off my muddy sneakers and stretched my aching legs out onto the stone hearth. Only ten a.m. and I was wiped. And I was due to give the new guests a talk about the ranch cuisine in two hours!

"You're stealing my warmth."

I turned and smiled at Allison, seated behind me. "I didn't notice you back there. You're practically lost in that sofa."

Behind me in the huge raftered sitting room, ringing the central stone fireplace, were leather chairs and a heavily cushioned, eight-foot-long brown leather sofa. Stretched out across its entire length was a very languorous Allison in a purple warm-up suit. Her silky blonde hair was pulled back into a twist and secured by a gold comb. Gold hoop earrings completed the cool, polished look, but the mud-encrusted track shoes on the floor beside the sofa testified that Allison did more than just drape herself in glamorous poses.

"Just shove over a touch, lamb. Carlos'll turn up any minute and throw on another log."

I got up and pushed my chair a bit to the side, no longer blocking the fire.

"What have you been up to?" I asked. "I didn't see you as I

trudged through the meadow this morning, so I guess you took the high road."

"Weeeeell, tell you the truth, I slept in this morning. Six months of Sturm und Drang caught up with me."

"What kind of Sturm?"

"I've been real busy making money. Lots of it. I'm a real estate broker in Tucson. Got my own firm. And I'm a sometime developer. Now, don't look so stunned. I'm brighter than I look."

I winced. "It's just that I pictured you as a model or boutique owner. Or as the very pampered society wife of a multimillionaire tycoon."

"Matter of fact, I've been a model, and matter of fact, the very pampered society wife of a tycoon, too, but he was just a millionaire. Now I pamper myself—and I'm fixing to beat him to the next million. Or three."

Allison swung her long legs from the sofa and sat up, stretching. She held her hands out to the fire, turning the emerald ring on her right hand to and fro admiringly.

"He never bought me anything I didn't pay for, one way or the other."

"Do you have children?"

"No ma'am, but not for lack of trying." She stared at the flames. "I remember reading somewhere that there were only two things in life that become obsessions when you don't have them—money and children. I'm working on the money now, but I've given up on the children."

"Phooey. You can't be more than thirty-six, thirty-seven. About my age. There's time for both of us."

Allison smiled. "Phooey yourself. You're a mighty good writer, Nora, and probably a terrific cooking teacher. But you're a rotten judge of age. You're almost a decade off. My time's run out." She patted the cushion beside her. "Come tell me more about you. Talk to me."

I moved over and, somewhat to my surprise, talked to her. I'd quit psychotherapy three years back, and so I'd lost the habit of talking about myself. No, that wasn't true, was it? It was more that Max had been my closest friend, and with him out of my life, there were few people with whom to share my innermost thoughts.

So I talked to this new friend about the excitement and fun— and the dyspepsia and deadlines—involved in reviewing restaurants and cookbooks for a weekly magazine; about writing columns, ghostwriting a celebrity cookbook, and teaching baking classes. With more difficulty, I even talked a bit about the estrangement between Max and me.

"I think Max got custody of my mother," I said. "She's wild about him. Rose is an old-line unreconstructed liberal from the sixties, a social worker. Very politically connected. Bella Abzug was her dearest friend. She and my dad—he died some years ago. He was a high school principal—expected me to do 'socially significant' work. Rose was heartsick when I said I wanted to be a chef."

"How in heaven's name did you ever get involved with food?"

"Rose was a horrific cook when she was around to try. She was so busy saving the world when I was a kid, it was either learn to cook or live at Burger King." I smiled, remembering the weekends when she was off marching or attending conferences and my dad and I would wander through New York, eating everything in sight. I'd slip menus into my backpack and experiment in my free time. He was my best audience; thought everything I did—and cooked—was fabulous.

"I stuck it out through college," I explained to Allison, "but took the money Dad left me when he died and went to the Culinary Institute in Hyde Park. He'd have approved. Let someone else save the world."

"Is Max into food, too?"

"Can you believe it, he's a picky eater."

Allison laughed. "So why is Rose so enamored of him?"

"Ah, he's saving the world in his own way. He's a straight arrow: Yale Law School, the U.S. Attorney's office. He's in charge of the Major Crime Unit in Manhattan. Rose would rather he was a poor defense lawyer, but at least he's on the side of truth and justice."

"Is he on your side?" asked Allison.

I didn't answer right away—couldn't.

"He really does love me," I finally said. "I think. We were together nearly three years. But we drove each other crazy. He likes a calm, predictable life, likes to be in control. Of course, he says I like to be in control, too. And that I'm a loose cannon, that I jump into the pool without checking that it's got water. Calls me grandiose—says I think I really do know what's best for everybody. I guess I'm more my mother's daughter than not. We both have a strong tendency to meddle."

"It's not finished, is it?"

"Damn, I hope not. Who else would eat Mallomars with me in bed, listening to schmaltzy Italian operas? As well as to Mississippi blues."

Allison smiled at me. "An unbeatable combination."

"I feel as though I'm back at Vassar, talking about last night's date. How come you're not, as they say, sharing?"

"I've shared more than my usual." Allison smiled again, to take the edge off her words, but I knew she meant them. She knocked the mud off her sneakers and laced them up, then stood, checking her watch.

" 'Live in the here,' those New Agers say, and 'the here' here has to do with abominable abdominals. Come on; we've missed one class. Let's catch this next one."

I hesitated. What I really wanted to do was finish reading

Margaret Maron's latest mystery; I'd fallen asleep with it open on my lap.

I said, "I can't even find my abs. They're in hiding. But when I do find them, I'll certainly speak to them about that class."

"Wimp. Gotta run. See you at lunch."

"No lunch for me. I'm fasting."

"Oh, I forgot. Poor lamb. How was your morning pick-me-up?"

"Not too bad. Some sort of foamy brew that vaguely resembled a malted, a slug of potassium in an orange drink, and two vitamins. CeCe was there. At least a dozen other brave souls. All women. No surprise there. They called your pal Alan's name, but he was a no-show."

"Really? Curious. He always fasts . . . for a couple of days. Then he gets bored. Well, this time maybe he got bored just thinking about it."

Allison turned and floated from the room. I struggled getting up from the depths of the couch and edged back into my damp sneakers. Another few minutes in front of the fire and I'd lose all will to move.

CHAPTER FIVE

Later Sunday morning

The sitting room had become more crowded while Allison and I were talking, and I smiled politely to several of the women I recognized from the morning walks and my lectures. It was quite a mélange: fitness junkie couples, several mothers and grown daughters, wealthy socialites who flit from spa to spa, a number of women needing to lose weight. I could certainly relate to that group! I was concentrating so hard on walking with my shoulders back, abdominals tucked in, and tailbone down that I barely noticed Jody Neel across the room, walking slowly and carefully, trying to balance a cup of tea along with her turquoise tote bag. A few feet from me, she stumbled. Her tea, her very hot tea, splashed over her and everyone in her vicinity. Including me.

"Oh, gosh, I'm so sorry!" cried Jody, her voice a loud whisper. "All over your tights! You're soaking. Oh God, I hope I didn't burn you. Let me get some paper towels . . ."

"No, don't worry," I said. "It's okay. Just an accident."

"So careless of me . . ."

"Don't worry about it. Really." I smiled reassuringly at the nervous young woman, who was dabbing ineffectually at both of us with a soggy napkin.

"I wasn't really watching where I was going. It's Nora, isn't it? I'm just so edgy. You know, about my friend Alan Nardy. No one knows where he's gone to, and I can't help worrying. I peeked in his cottage window. His suitcase is open, on the bed, so he got here. I even checked the parking lot, and his BMW's there."

I mumbled some platitude about putting it out of her mind, and suggested I get us some fresh tea. When I finally settled down on a window seat with Jody and two chamomile teas, I asked, "Why are you so sure something's happened to your friend? Isn't it possible that what your husband suggested at dinner last night is right? That Alan's found a woman he wants to be with, alone?"

"Simon's not the best judge of this," said Jody, more quietly now. "He's somewhat irrational about Alan. I met Alan a long time ago, when I used to come here with my mother. He was so sweet to me. I adored him. We even talked about maybe, you know, maybe getting married. But Mother was always afraid he was just interested in . . ."

She stopped abruptly, clearly uncomfortable with having revealed so much to a stranger. But her unlikely relationship to sexy Simon made a kind of cynical sense to me now: Jody must be one rich young lady.

She held on to the cup of tea with both hands, then visibly shook herself into another mode.

"I'm going back to the room to change, and you should really change out of those wet tights, Nora."

"I intend to. I have to pick up some work in my room, anyway."

I turned to hunt for my windbreaker, then looked over to the door as it was thrown open with great force.

CeCe stood in the open doorway. Her eyes were red and swollen, her tiny gamine face twisted with grief.

"He's dead."

"No," whispered Jody, dropping the cup and holding out her hand as if to push the words away. She didn't ask whom CeCe meant. She didn't need to.

"He's dead," CeCe repeated, still not moving from the door. "On the mountain." There was shocked silence in the room. Simon appeared behind CeCe and pushed past her to reach Jody. He put his hands on her rigid shoulders.

"Jode. Baby . . ."

"Don't. Don't pretend you care. You don't even like him. I love him! I loved him before I even knew you!" Jody began to wail, and Simon looked helplessly at me, still standing frozen beside Jody in the middle of the room.

"What did CeCe mean, on the mountain?" I asked Simon. "How could he be dead on the mountain?"

"They found him on the slope near Sultan's Cap," said Simon carefully. "He must have tripped, fallen. Hit his head. They think he's been dead for hours." Simon hesitated. "I was in Dolores's office when they brought him down on a stretcher. He was a mess. Some animals got to him . . ." He finally broke off, mindful at last of Jody's stunned horror.

CeCe finally moved away from the doorway and came to Jody, tears welling up in her eyes.

"I loved him too, Jody darling. Come on, dear heart, sit down by the fire. I'll tell you the little I know."

Jody nodded her head, sobbing and rocking back and forth on the sofa. Now there was a low buzz behind us, as the news passed quickly around the room. Simon stood to the side of the sofa, watching his wife.

CeCe, stroking Jody's hair, said, "Seems someone found Alan's ski cap on the trail before breakfast and turned it in to the concierge's desk. Dolores was on duty and recognized it. Hard not to. You know the one, red, with a turquoise band and little turquoise pom-pom on top? Clashed something awful with that parka of his. She knew he was missing . . . we'd all been carrying on so, looking all over for him, so she got spooked.

Worried that maybe he was hurt, stuck on the mountain." CeCe paused and thought about her words. "Guess we were all right to worry."

"What could have happened?" I asked Simon quietly.

He shrugged. "There'll be some sort of investigation, maybe even an autopsy. Probably died of a cerebral hemorrhage, exposure, something like that. Dolores said he was partially hidden in the brush. All morning, people must have marched up and down that bloody trail, nobody noticed. He probably fell some time late yesterday."

"How could he . . ."

"Jesus, Nora, I don't know any more than I told you. Dolores is my only source, and she's mostly carrying on about her job—'It's not my responsibility; guests are warned never to climb alone, why did he go up so late in the day?' All that shit."

"You can't really blame Dolores," I said righteously. I didn't know Alan—and didn't particularly like what I'd heard about him—but I was temporary staff here and could see Dolores's point. "She's probably worried about the ranch getting sued for negligence," I explained, "or herself getting fired, or just as bad, the story getting into the papers. An accidental death on a mountaintop's not exactly the best publicity for a health spa."

Simon didn't bother answering me. He moved to the fireplace and poked at the huge logs with the iron tool resting on the stone ledge. Without looking at his wife, he asked, "You all cried out, Jode? Let's go up to the villa. You can rest there."

"You go, Simon," she said. "I'm staying with CeCe for a bit."

"Tell you the truth, Jody honey," said CeCe, mopping her eyes, "I think I need some alone time. I just can't believe it's true. And I'd sure like to know who walked up that mountain with him. No way would Alan go up alone. Y'all know how he hated to climb. He always said he needed to talk his way up."

"Is Dolores calling Mariana to tell her?" asked Jody. "That

witch! She's so patronizing to Mariana. Maybe if she hasn't called yet . . ."

"She's telling Mariana's brothers. They'll call her. I thought maybe Allison would offer. She and Alan were real close, but she just walked away when we all found out. I guess she needed to be alone."

"If Alan fell yesterday and was on the mountain all night," said Jody, wincing a bit at the thought, "who did Nora hear moving around in his cottage?"

CHAPTER SIX

Monday midday

Most of the new guests showed up for my noon class about the ranch food plan, but very few paid any attention. I struggled upstream against buzz about Alan Nardy's death. It was hardly surprising, even though none of us knew him personally. I was itching to know more about the accident, too. What a bizarre happening, particularly since the victim was a frequent visitor, ostensibly aware of the hiking rules and familiar with the trails. I felt sad for Allison and her friends, but was unembarrassed to admit that most of my concern was personal: how was this man's death going to affect the ranch, and my own agenda here? Would there be articles in travel and spa journals? Cancellations? More stringent rules about hiking? Maybe even some firing (oh, yes please, let's lose Dolores!).

I managed to get through my talk and the few questions that followed, then dropped by the lodge for my midday "meal": a small cup of cold cucumber soup, a second small cup of nuts and seeds, and a tall glass of iced herbal tea. As I walked into the sitting room, I saw CeCe just leaving. I wasn't sure she saw me.

Somehow Alan's death, and everyone's reaction to it, was intensifying my sense of aloneness. Perhaps, I thought, that's why I'd glommed onto Allison and CeCe. I wandered around the sitting room, nodding to the few women I recognized, but no one invited me to join them. *Don't feel sorry for yourself,*

Franke! Do something! Incredibly restless, I stood irresolute for some minutes, then decided to go to the ranch kitchen, my home away from home, until the afternoon classes started. There was always work I could do there.

The kitchen was a blessed sea of calm. This was a rare enough experience anywhere on the ranch, but particularly in the kitchen, where organized chaos was the rule. Of course, it was after lunch and before the dinner prep. Not even Miguel was around. I sat down at my so-called desk, just a card table tucked into a corner of the kitchen that I'd fitted out with a file holder and cookbooks, and dug out my predecessor Marya's folder of recipes. She was a humorless nutritionist, and since she'd be returning after her maternity leave, I didn't want to shake up her system.

I really was getting sick of the mostly vegetarian menus. While the vegetables were organic and wonderfully fresh—in fact, most of the ones we used were grown on the farm adjacent to the spa—and I loved the salads and pureed soups, I didn't come naturally to vegetarian cuisine. Even the two nights a week of fish and the delicate fruit desserts didn't help. If we could only vary the menu more. Maybe I could adapt my favorite Mediterranean dish, chicken-with-almonds-and-apricots, to fish. I'd need something meaty to stand up to the soy-and-apricot sauce. Possibly mahimahi, or mako. I'd need to check with Miguel about availability, and make sure we had sliced almonds and dried apricots on hand. Perhaps prunes as well. Although that would surely raise the calorie count.

As for a side dish, on my visit to the farm yesterday (I found it helped to have a goal in walking), I'd noticed some baby arugula. We could use it in a salad, of course, which is what Miguel usually did, but maybe he could be persuaded to flavor one of his pasta or rice dishes with the piquant greens, and add some pignoli and a touch of feta cheese.

Playing with the recipes had accomplished my goal: I felt calmer and more mellow. But hungry! Could I . . . would I . . . break my liquid fast with just a little something? I stood, preparing to raid the walk-in refrigerator, when I heard heavy footsteps. I whirled around in a panic, then gasped with relief when I recognized the chef.

"*Hola*, Miguel. I'm so glad to see you!"

That wasn't entirely true. While I'd been alarmed at the possibility of an intruder in the kitchen and was therefore relieved to see the burly, mustachioed man, my relationship with Miguel has deteriorated these last few days. Most of my first week he'd been charmingly flirtatious, but lately he'd been cool and sarcastic.

I had tried to inject pleasure into my voice, but I knew that Miguel resented me and would fight me on any menu change.

"Señorita Franke," he said, standing over me. He oozed disapproval. "May I help you, *por favor?*"

I stiffened. I was perfectly within my rights to be in the kitchen, with or without *Señor* Miguel. He needn't make me feel like an interloper.

"Please call me Nora, Miguel," as I had so often asked these past weeks. "I was thinking about some changes to the menu," I said, as sweetly as possible. "Do you have a few minutes to discuss them with me?"

"The menu is firm for the next many weeks, *Señorita*. There is no need to disturb yourself to change it."

He hovered over me, scowling, as he tried to read my notes sitting on the table.

"Too sweet," he said. "Like dessert."

"What are you talking about?"

"This fish. Apricots. Prunes. Do you want also whipped cream?"

"Miguel, don't be mean." I actually simpered. I might make

41

myself sick. "This is a perfectly legitimate recipe, flavored with garlic and onions as well as the fruit. It's even low in fat. But if you wish, you could spice it up. Maybe add cilantro, to balance the sweetness. Give it some kick."

He didn't answer right away. Finally, he gave a mighty shrug and sighed.

"If that is what you wish, *Señorita*. I will think upon it."

"And the arugula and feta salad," I said, in a disgustingly wheedling voice.

He nodded and took the recipes I handed him. I decided to leave while I was ahead. There was a Pilates class I'd promised myself as a treat. Amazing how my notion of "treats" had changed since my arrival at the ranch.

CHAPTER SEVEN

Monday evening

I shivered a bit in the fading sunlight, feeling the cold from the stone bench seep through my new navy velour warm-up suit. I had thought I might regret not dressing more warmly for the sunset hour on Allison's terrace, but I couldn't resist showing off my purchases. Happily, the boutique recognized that not all spa-goers are a size eight. Or ten. Or fourteen.

Our hostess had been deeply immersed in conversation with Phoebe, the PR specialist, since my arrival, leaving me feeling stranded. CeCe hadn't appeared, and while I'd met the others, I didn't have any real relationship with them. All I could hear was Alan Nardy's name. Of course, he had been a regular in their ranch visits, possibly a onetime love interest of Allison as well as Jody. His death had cast a pall over everything and everybody today, not just this group of his closest friends.

Since I hadn't known him, while I was shocked, I couldn't share my new friends' anguish. And truthfully, I was getting tired of the subject. I ran through a mental checklist. I was happy about my work during the last two weeks here: my talks and demonstrations were well attended, and I was making progress updating the menus. I wasn't thrilled with how cool Miguel had been at this afternoon's unexpected meeting, though. My mind wandered over any tactless criticisms I may have made, any overt challenges to his authority. The changes I recommended in the menus are probably challenge enough, I concluded.

Physically I was feeling pretty good. Not instantly thin, as I'd magically hoped. Less bloated, certainly. The little gold-and-onyx antique ring my Tanta Basha gave me on my sixteenth birthday, which I'd been unable to remove from my pinkie for the last two years, was flopping over on its side. I'd certainly be in better shape for my fourth-floor walk-up when I got home.

I missed my apartment. I'd transformed the once-gracious front room of a Victorian townhouse into an office/living room, overseen by my Burmese cat, Sable, whose domain was the cozy window seat Max had built into the bay window overlooking Riverside Park and the Hudson River. The bedroom and bath were minuscule, but I'd exercised all my ingenuity and bank account on the pocket kitchen. No full-scale suburban kitchen boasted better equipment! Not to mention a marble work surface for pastry making and hardwood chopping areas bleached from constant scrubbing. I could only hope that my sublet tenant Leslie—a colleague at *MetroScene*—was cherishing the apartment, and Sable.

"I've been looking for you all day!"

CeCe stood frowning down at me, her voice tense and accusatory.

"Hey, CeCe, I'm glad you're here. I guess our 'drink times' didn't coincide today."

"Guess it'll have to wait till we're alone," she continued without seeming even to hear me. She grabbed the hand of a tall, rangy man who must have arrived with her, and introduced us.

"Nora, you remember Tom Rappaport? He was at dinner last night. He wanted to say 'hi' to you."

I smiled a hello, surprised that actually I didn't remember having met him. I must have really been distracted last night;

this was not someone I'd ordinarily overlook. He wasn't precisely handsome, but was interesting-looking, craggy in a Sam Shepard kind of way.

"You look like you smoke a pipe." I said.

"I used to. But never here."

Tom seemed perfectly comfortable with my non sequitur. I liked that; Max always questioned my questions.

He smiled, then raised a finger to indicate he'd be right back, and went over to the makeshift bar to pour a drink.

Uh-oh, I thought, acutely aware of an anticipatory flutter in my body. This was not part of my game plan.

I watched Tom exchange greetings with Simon, who had detached himself from Jody to join him at the bar. Simon, resplendent in a gray cashmere pullover and ironed (ironed!) faded jeans, was holding an icy vodka and tonic and looking serious and worldly, like a full-page liquor ad in *GQ*. Tom, I thought, warming to my magazine fantasy, was more suited to a picture essay on "keeping fit after forty" in *Sports Illustrated*. He was dressed in the male version of the ranch uniform—jogging pants, a sweatshirt proclaiming "Columbia University," worn track shoes. He looked slightly disheveled, sweaty. And disconcertingly masculine. At least I felt reassured that my hormones were still operational.

He sat down beside me and took a big gulp of his beer, looking amiably at me. I felt my body warm and soften. Ah Max, it's been too long.

"I'd better not sit too close," he said finally. "I don't exactly smell like a rose."

I sniffed theatrically. "Jock Number Five."

He had pulled off his sweatshirt and I was very conscious of the grayish-black hair curling over the top of his T-shirt, and of the hard thigh muscles tensed beneath the soft drape of his jogging pants.

"Do you teach there?" I asked, motioning to his Columbia University sweatshirt.

"My daughter's a sophomore there," he answered. "I'm a veep at an ad agency. I work with the account guys."

"Out here?" I asked. "In California?"

"God no, in New York. I live in Connecticut . . . Stamford. I keep thinking of moving into the city but I'm a creature of habit." He moved around restlessly. "I feel weird hitting on you so soon after hearing about Alan. Not that that makes any sense, mind you. But I've been coming here since my divorce—nearly ten years now—and used to play tennis with Alan every year."

I was amused at how economically Tom communicated. Now I knew he was a long-term divorcé, had a young adult daughter, was successful enough to live in a ritzy suburb, and worked in the city. And was hitting on me!

"I wouldn't have figured you for a spa-goer," I commented.

"I travel a lot for business, but when I want a week to de-stress, I like it better here than at a glitzy resort. I can always find enough guys for a basketball or tennis game, and the weight room's great. I come every year at this time, with Allison's so-called posse."

Tom looked up at the tiny redhead wandering restlessly around the patio. "Stop pacing, Ceece. You're making even me nervous."

"I just wish y'all would take me seriously. I keep telling you that it was totally unlike Alan to climb the mountain on his own, much less before he made the rounds of the ranch checking everything out, setting up his massage appointments, greeting all of us. He liked to work up to the mountain. He'd never run up there right off the bat. And he hated being alone. Something's fishy. Someone must have been with him. Least at first. Someone must have seen him! I just don't know how y'all can chat and flirt, and not think about darling Alan . . ."

"Don't do that, Phoebe," Allison snapped. "It's like chalk on a blackboard."

Phoebe, who had pulled out an elegant makeup kit from her tote bag and had started to buff her nails, looked at Allison with surprise but put away the emery board.

"I'm meeting Joe at the spa building," she said. "We're having dinner at the staff table. I'll ask around. Maybe someone saw him check in." She pulled out a black lacquer mirror from the makeup bag, fluffed out her billowing hair, and narrowed her eyes speculatively. Selecting a mascara wand and green eyeliner pencil, she slowly and meticulously touched up her eye makeup.

"You're great at that," I said. "Of course, you start with terrific green eyes."

Phoebe zipped up her makeup kit. "I start with terrific green contact lenses."

"Phoebe!" CeCe shrieked, her angst about Alan momentarily forgotten. "I'd no idea! I thought your eyes were truly green."

"So they are. A truly insipid green. I am not insipid. So I just help them along." She looked at me critically. "You really needn't do a thing about your eyes. . . . They're a nice dark blue. And big. But your brows are too heavy. You can get them shaped at the salon. And you could use blusher. Slims the face."

"One more week of no salt, and gallons of water, and Nora's cheekbones will be sharp enough to stab you in the heart," said Allison.

Phoebe shrugged, gathering up her belongings and standing.
"Adiós, amigos."

"I just cannot picture them together," CeCe whispered, although Phoebe was by now well out of earshot. "She must be three inches taller than Joe! And she wears high-heeled boots!"

"I'm sure she takes her boots off in bed," said Allison. She fluffed up CeCe's red curls and grinned. She had, unaccountably, recovered her good humor, and now began clearing away the cocktail paraphernalia. CeCe jumped up to help, waving me off, and I wandered over to the fence, where Tom was looking out at the mountain foothills in the distance.

There were still some clusters of fat black grapes clinging to the knobby, twisted vines that stretched for miles in neat, orderly rows. The vineyard was framed by a border of feathery olive trees, and beyond these, the fields were strewn with what I'd learned were stocky chaparral shrubs, flattop buckwheat, and aromatic California sage. Here and there clumps of Pacific lavender and the white flowers of coyote brush enlivened the landscape, and standing tall and messy among the ground-hugging succulents and shrubs were waving strands of . . .

"Pot!" I cried. "Marijuana. That's what those plants are! We're in a field of cannabis!"

CHAPTER EIGHT

Later Monday evening

Tom laughed. "Shhh," he said. "The grapevines might be wired."

"Surely we're not the only ones who can recognize cannabis. Anyone who grew up in the seventies and eighties . . . And what about those police roaming around, checking on Alan's death?"

"It's more a question of acknowledging than recognizing."

"Who's growing the stuff? Surely not my holistic employers?"

"Most of the land out there is leased by locals—mainly by the Cerillos—Alan Nardy's in-laws, in fact. They used to farm those fields in the foothills until they discovered a more profitable cash crop, and now they control a big chunk of the mountain. They don't precisely suggest that they'll interfere with the ranch hikes on the mountain if too much notice is taken, but it's understood."

"Does everyone know?"

"I doubt that anyone 'knows' officially," said Tom. "Alan mentioned to me, and probably to others, that some of Mariana's family are successful farmers. In fact, he advised them on investments. He was a financial adviser, you know." I nodded, mostly interested in keeping him talking to me. "Mariana's family's rumored to actually own most of the land roundabout. Of course, some still work here. The ranch is a major employer in this part of Baja."

Tom put his sweatshirt back on. "You look cold. And I'm starving. Let's go down to dinner. Tonight's a fish night, right?"

"Right, local shrimp, with tomatoes and tofu disguised as feta. Don't tell. But I'm not eating with you," I added. "I've got a small glass of some thickish drink to look forward to. CeCe should be joining me."

"Want to check out the movie later? It's some Goldie Hawn comedy. Or can I interest you in bridge?"

"I'll pass on the movie. And I haven't played bridge since college. But I'm good at kibitzing."

"I'll look for you over at the lodge after dinner," said Tom. "We'll think of something." He wandered over to the door of the villa and called to Allison and CeCe to get a move on.

I stuffed my hands in the pockets of my jacket and wondered about the "something" he was thinking of. The "something" I knew I wasn't ready to think of. I certainly was feeling very estranged from Max, and a tiny bit thinner, but not that estranged, and not that thin.

"CeCe, let's go!" I cried, suddenly impatient. "God forbid we should miss our dinner drink."

"Not to worry." CeCe came out of the villa, running her fingers through her curls and slipping on a pink suede jacket.

Tonight CeCe looked like an assortment of sorbets—plum sweatshirt and tights, strawberry hair, watermelon sandals.

"Patti pays attention to just who's missing," she said. "She'll save our drinks for us. She'll probably even label them with our names. Least, she's done that in the past." She tucked her hand in the crook of my arm and hugged it to her side.

"Been waiting all day to talk to you, Nora. I'm so confused about something Alan said . . ." Her eyes filled with tears.

"What was he really like, CeCe?" I asked, wanting to prevent further tears. "I know Simon has suggested he was quite a ladies' man." We started to walk down the hill toward the center of the ranch.

"Nonsense. He's just jealous that Jody knew Alan before him.

Alan was . . ." She paused, thinking about what she wanted to say. ". . . Alan just loved being with women, Nora. He flirted a lot, but I'm not really sure how much he actually did. Y'see, he'd get so excited about everything! He loved meeting new people, and telling his stories, and doing business deals . . . I once heard him making a pitch for new business in the hot tub!"

"He was successful, then?"

"Well, I guess. I mean, he always spent money like water. Buddy said he just talked a good game. And maybe he was right. Once I missed my plane in San Diego, and I stopped by Alan's office to take him to lunch. It wasn't much of an office, you know. Not very classy. But he always had lots of plans. Allison?"

CeCe twisted around so she could see Allison and Tom, who were walking behind us on the narrow path. "Didn't you and Alan talk about setting up some sort of investment thing together?"

"Talked about it," agreed Allison. "Alan liked to talk."

"He liked to live well, too. Champagne taste," said Tom. "Champagne and caviar."

"Me too," I said. "Nothing wrong with caviar."

"You just have to visit Buddy and me, Nora. His mama's cook, Samantha, cooks for us now, and she's right famous for her Texas caviar."

"Which is?"

"Pickled black-eyed peas. Don't y'all laugh! Then she makes Texas-style chili—with red-hot chilies! And it's got venison and suet and cornmeal in it, along with pinto beans and rice and . . ."

"Not fair!" cried Tom. "You're tormenting a starving man. Knock off the food talk."

"Come on over to the dining room after your drink, CeCe, Nora," called out Allison, as she led Tom off at a fast clip toward the lodge. "I heard there's going to be some sort of memorial thing for Alan. Too little, too late."

"What does that mean?" I asked CeCe.

CeCe looked troubled as she held the door open for us. The smells and sounds of a crackling wood fire greeted us and, momentarily overcome with nostalgia for other fires, other times, I didn't catch CeCe's response.

CHAPTER NINE

Monday evening, later

There were only a dozen or so people still milling around in the huge sitting room, but as CeCe had promised, there were still a few drinks and tiny containers of seeds left on the corner table. I noticed Allison and Tom hovering over a table of picked-over crudités and my latest yogurt-based herb dip, chatting with a few of the "cocktail-hour" stragglers. While CeCe went off to the ladies' room, I picked up the two paper cups with my name on them (the main course and side dish!) and moved toward the windows, away from the others, ready to be alone for a moment.

I sipped the viscous liquid slowly, trying not to think about the cloyingly sweet taste of my almond milk "dinner" and pathetically grateful for the tiny seeds to chew. It was hard to believe it was only Monday night, and only the beginning of my third week; I felt I'd been at the ranch forever. It was a bit like being on a long voyage at sea. We were all thrown together onboard ship and formed relationships that might have taken months to develop on land. Now I understood the derivation of "in the same boat."

The liquid fast made for a change. I did miss the easy camaraderie of the dinner table and would miss it even more now that Tom had appeared on the scene, but it was fun sharing the experience with CeCe and a few of the other women I was getting to know. I was surprisingly satisfied as far as the drinks themselves were concerned.

"Lunch" yesterday had been the decided winner: one small glass of delectable chilled gazpacho, made from finely chopped tomatoes, cucumbers, green pepper, onions, mint, parsley. No oil, of course, and—I was reasonably certain—no other liquid. The moisture in the tomatoes and onions were surely enough to have liquefied the gazpacho somewhat. I needed to speak to Miguel about the exact ingredients, so I could adapt it as a cold soup for the guest menu.

"How're you doing, lady?" chirped Patti, the impossibly cheery staff nutritionist, startling me by appearing suddenly at my elbow with a tray full of paper cups.

"I'm doing just fine, thank you, Patti."

I forced myself to smile. By now, Patti had to know how irritating I found it to be called "lady." But it had been made abundantly clear to me, by Patti, by Miguel, and by Dolores, the ranch manager, that my presence as menu consultant was unwelcome.

"Right. Drinking lots of water I hope," bubbled Patti, offering me one of the cups on the tray. I exchanged my empty glass of almond milk for the water.

"Enough so that I pee constantly," I admitted.

"Good girl. Water for sale, water for sale!"

Sipping the water, I wandered around the room, smiling and eavesdropping as I went. Not surprisingly, Alan's death was still the subject of most of the conversation. The consensus seemed to be that as tragic as it was, the accident had been his own fault. Everyone was warned never to climb the mountain alone. There were snakes (although they supposedly emerged only at high noon, to take the sun), the possibility of sprained ankles, of taking a wrong turn. Even on group hikes, there was always a staff member who acted as "shepherd," complete with first aid equipment, to follow the last straggler. Usually me.

I noticed wryly that everyone (including me) was eager to absolve the ranch from any responsibility in Alan's death. It was certainly easy to fall under its spell, I thought. There was something about the reverence for the pure and natural—in food, landscaping, even (except for CeCe) personal dress—that intensified the feeling of being on a physical and mental retreat from the real world.

At some point during my wanderings, Allison and Tom must have left for dinner. Out of the corner of my eye I noticed CeCe reenter the room. She was in her usual state of breathless energy, red curls bouncing, long purple sweatshirt glued to shiny purple tights. She swirled around like a mini tornado, throwing out greetings, then alighted at the corner table where the one drink remained.

"Told you they'd save our drinks." CeCe called out to me, searching around for a place to stash her overflowing pink tote bag. She beckoned to me to come closer.

Her mobile little face suddenly changed dramatically, looking at once tragic and secretive.

"Finally we have a chance to talk privately," CeCe said, with an air of heavy mystery. "I mean, it was so unlike Alan. Just doesn't make sense at all. And I can't understand why she insisted . . ."

"Which of you girls is Nora Franke?"

I winced at the "girls," and at the interruption, and turned to find an older woman with heavy-duty wrinkles and a long gray braid whom I had noticed in my low-impact aerobics class that afternoon. I had wondered about the wisdom of the ranch permitting a woman who had to be at least seventy to follow its rigorous program, but three minutes into the warm-up I'd been disabused of that concern. The woman was a pretzel, lithe and flexible and with more endurance than half the class.

"I'm Nora."

"Dorothy Kazantian." She was brisk and businesslike. "I have a ten thirty massage tomorrow I need to change, and they told me at the desk that you want to switch from the afternoon."

I nodded and turned to look for my loaded tote bag. Like most of the guests, I carried with me a bathing suit, light windbreaker, my beauty and class schedules. In addition, I had notes on the menu and recipe ideas. It was heavy and a jumble. As I rummaged through it to find my massage tickets, I turned back to CeCe, to ask her to wait a moment longer.

She was still standing where I had left her. She was uncommonly pale and had a bewildered expression on her face.

"CeCe, you okay?"

She didn't answer and swayed slightly. As I hesitated, uncertain as to what to do, CeCe doubled over and dropped her glass, spilling what little liquid was left on the tile floor. She moaned—a child's moan, frightened and defenseless—and clutched her belly, then crumpled onto the floor and curled into a fetal position. I ran over and fell on my knees beside CeCe and awkwardly reached out to her.

"Ohmigod, CeCe, are you okay? Gas pains?"

My words echoed in the suddenly silent room.

"Let's get her to the nurse's office—someone call Phyllis and tell her we're on our way. Might be appendicitis." Dorothy took charge crisply, scooping up the moaning CeCe in her arms as if she were a small child and starting for the door.

I felt momentarily resentful of her bossiness, then ran to the phone at the far end of the room and jingled the button impatiently for the operator. But before anyone came on the line, I was riveted by a scream.

"Look at her! Do something!" shrieked a young woman, scarcely out of her teens, grabbing the arm of the woman standing next to her. Turning back to the door, I saw that CeCe was rigid, her body arched in a spasm. I dropped the phone and ran to help Dorothy, who had fallen to her knees in an effort to hold on to CeCe. CeCe retched and then vomited, and Dorothy released her to the floor hastily, trying to escape the vomit. CeCe's arms flailed wildly at tortured angles from her body; her mouth dropped open in a soundless scream; her eyes stared into the abyss.

No one in the room moved.

This is not happening, I thought.

Dorothy wiped her hands and clothing carefully with a towel that had been lying on a nearby chair, never taking her eyes off CeCe's face. She placed the tips of her fingers along the artery on CeCe's neck, then laid her head down on CeCe's chest and listened to her heart. Gently, she pressed CeCe's eyelids closed.

CHAPTER TEN

Monday night, later

I don't remember much about the next few hours. I do remember that someone shoved me into a chair and gave me a glass of water. That someone else pulled me toward the bathroom when it became clear I was going to throw up. After I washed my face, I came back out and just sat. Numb and shaky.

I sat alone and silent until some nervous young uniformed officers, probably from nearby Almagro, knelt by my side and tried to question me. My Spanish, and their English, just wasn't up to the challenge. I sat quietly some more.

Finally, one of the other women noticed me shaking and got me a blanket. Someone wrapped me up and I gradually became calmer. But I continued to sit in a daze.

It seemed like all night, but could only have been an hour or so, before the police found Dolores and had her interpret for Dorothy, myself, and the others in the sitting room. I managed to pull myself together to answer questions, although I was vaguely aware of tears falling unceasingly down my face. Finally, they brought in the big gun, an Inspector Enrique Nuñez. He was in a truly splendid uniform and spoke broken English, and he repeated all the questions all over again. By this time I had a fierce headache and wanted to lie down. I must have said as much, because I was led next door to a cold, cavernous room and left alone.

CHAPTER ELEVEN

Monday night, even later

I woke from a disturbed, disorienting sleep. I felt numb and somewhat dopey. I looked at my watch. Five after ten. Only three hours had passed since CeCe . . . no, don't go there. I couldn't get my mind around the idea that CeCe was dead. That she'd died in front of my eyes, while I'd flailed around helplessly. I'd never seen a dead person before; I was ashamed of my revulsion and heartsick about CeCe.

Where was everyone? It was too damned quiet in here. What was happening next door? Had everyone else been questioned and sent away? I felt impatient with my passivity. I wanted to know what was happening, dammit. I moved quickly to the door, then stood there, irresolute.

Did I really want to go back into the sitting room? What if CeCe was still lying frozen on the floor? Did I really want to see her body, smell the vomit on the floor, relive that horrific moment?

I recoiled as the door opened abruptly, then relaxed when I saw it was Allison.

"What's happening in there?" I asked, my voice choked with tears.

Allison beckoned me to the sofa, then pushed over a round leather hassock and sank down on it, her long legs crossed in front of her yoga-style. She was very pale, and her voice was even huskier than usual, as if she'd smoked too much or talked too long. Or cried?

"They wouldn't let me in here until now," said Allison. "They're . . . taking her away. They're finished here for tonight. Talked to just about everyone who'd wandered in and out of the lodge all night. Probably tomorrow we'll lose these local guys and get higher-ups, who'll ask more questions. Once they think about the tourists involved and the complications. We need to get some sleep."

"Are you kidding? I won't be able to sleep. What kinds of complications? Was it some sort of food poisoning? I thought at first it was an appendicitis attack. But you don't die from that."

Allison shrugged her shoulders and started to pull the long golden hairpins out of her chignon, letting her hair cascade down to her shoulders. She shook her hair until it hung loose, then ran her fingers through it to untangle the knots.

"If they know, they're not telling. At least, they're not telling us. They've been in touch with something called the *Servicio Médico Forense*—sounds to me like the medical examiner's office. Then I think they'll want to talk to us."

"First Alan's accident, now CeCe . . ."

"It does rather stretch the imagination to believe that two guests, friends, have died within a day of each other by coincidence. Let me point out," Allison continued, looking grim and irritable, "that Rancho de las Flores has been in operation for forty-something years. There've been some accidents, of course, broken bones and sprained ankles. I remember hearing some fool once had a heart attack after running up and down the mountain in August. Midday, no less. But no one ever fell off the mountain before. And certainly no one ever died during cocktail hour before. And these two 'nevers' never happened a day apart before, either. Or neither. I never get that straight."

I ignored her flippancy, choosing to believe she was chattering from nerves. But then, I'd known her for only a few days.

Maybe she didn't really care. Or cared too much.

"What now?" I asked.

"Well, I gather there's a long line forming outside the office and the phones. Lemmings racing toward planes and taxis to get the hell out of here. Panic time."

"Are you leaving? Would they even let us leave?"

"The police say no one can leave. Yet. Do you want to leave?"

I stared off into the distance, thinking about it. Dammit, no. I didn't want to leave. This was supposed to be my time, my chance to turn my life around.

"No. Oh, I don't know. I'm sick about CeCe, really sick. But I'm mad as hell to even have to think about leaving. Oh God, I feel so selfish."

Allison hooted. "You feel selfish! You should have seen that Dorothy person, trying to get in here to ask if you still want to switch tomorrow's massage appointment."

Allison unwound herself and stood, stretched her arms to the sky, then slowly curled down from the waist, reaching to her toes with her hands and her hair.

"First nod your head 'yes,' " she murmured, quoting, I realized, Joe's directions in his morning stretch class, "then shake your head 'no.' " She straightened up. "The 'noes' have it. Hard to believe that we haven't stumbled into the middle of some soap opera."

"What do the others think? Jody, Tom . . . do they think CeCe's death is related to Alan's? Wasn't his fall just an accident? Maybe CeCe was just an innocent victim. Or someone could be trying to discredit the ranch."

"Nobody knows what to think. We're all still in shock. If anything, we've been thinking about who's going to meet Buddy, CeCe's husband, at the airport in the morning. The local police inspector, a rather sour fellow named Enrique

Nuñez—looks like he has heartburn—he called Buddy and broke the news. In stilted, but painfully understandable English. Except, what's to understand? Damn, one of us should really meet him at the airport. He's arranging for a private jet to Tijuana. Dolores tried to foist that happy little job off on me, but I'm not having any. Maybe Tom'll do it—he's nicer than I am. Phoebe offered, but she's such an icicle she'd freeze him to death."

I watched Allison as she roamed around the room, rearranging chess pieces, stacking backgammon tiles, lining up billiard cues. I didn't try to stop the flow of Allison's thoughts or get her to sit down. I was remembering a rainy night last June, after Max suggested we not rent the Fire Island house together that summer, to give us each "space," and I had walked miles, clear from my apartment on the Upper West Side to Chinatown, weaving in and out of side streets, down Broadway, Fifth Avenue, the Bowery, unable to even stand still at corners until the red lights changed to green.

"If it's more than just accidents, like maybe an attempt to ruin the ranch," I said finally, "then CeCe—even Alan—may not have been the real target. It could have been anyone. That drink could have been meant for me. No, that's silly. Melodramatic. The drinks had our names on them, after all."

Allison looked at me. "Perhaps, if you're that worried, you should leave, Nora honey."

"Oh no, no, I'm staying. I've got a contract, got work to do here. And I'd much rather get poisoned than remain fat."

Allison threw back her head and laughed. She sank down on the hassock again and beamed at me.

"Oh, I can't tell you how you cheer me up. Everyone out there's being sanctimonious and weepy, and giving fake excuses for staying on. I'll be a truth teller, too. If I left here and went home now, I'd be obliged to pop in to the office, call my housekeeper back from her week off, deal with a beau or two I've been avoiding . . . much easier to stay the week like I planned. It was hard enough making arrangements to get here in the first place. Besides, this is all fantasy. No way they'll let us leave. We're stuck. At least for now."

"Am I interrupting?"

Jody was hovering in the doorway, draped against the ornately carved oak door. She was wearing a black turtleneck sweater and fashionably baggy jeans, but the black emphasized the pallor of her skin, and the jeans simply hung on her slight frame. Her lipstick had worn off, leaving her lips blotchy and undefined. The residue from mascara was smeared below Jody's reddened eyes. Her whole person seemed to droop in a forlorn, pathetic curve. She looked like a marionette with her strings loosened. I understood her misery but still wanted to shake her.

"Lordy, lordy," said Allison with exasperation. "You sure do look a treat. Come on in, girl. Stand up straight. Don't slouch. Where's that husband of yours?"

Tears welled up in Jody's eyes, clearly not for the first time that night.

"Simon's gone off to bed. Said he'd had it with high drama."

"Humph." Allison looked disapproving. "I know he disliked Alan intensely, but I thought he was fond of CeCe."

"He was, he was," sobbed Jody. "He called her 'an adorable fluff ball.' " She stopped crying suddenly, wiped her eyes with her sleeve. "Of course," she said, "it wasn't as if he knew her all that well."

"No? I thought he saw quite a bit of her when he was doing that plan for a new city outside of Dallas a couple of years back. Didn't Buddy invest a bit in that deal? Seems to me CeCe mentioned something about their real estate connections . . ."

"You must have misunderstood. They were the merest of acquaintances." Jody turned and fled the room.

"Well, well, well. The pussycat has claws," I murmured.

"More like a lioness protecting her lair, if you ask me," said Allison. "She sure did hasten to distance her beloved from the deceased. Come, Nora. It's way past our bedtime. You couldn't possibly look as bad as Jody, but it's not your finest hour. *Vámonos!*"

I followed Allison slowly out of the room. As we left the lodge, I could see groups of women huddled together, no one walking alone. There were radio taxis lined up at the bottom of the hill, but they were empty; probably no one was allowed to leave. My body was stiff, from tension as much as from the curled-up position in which I'd been sitting, and my head ached. I wanted Max. Wanted to talk to him, to tell him everything and have him make it make sense. Or just hug me. I wrapped my arms around my waist and hugged myself. Tight.

CHAPTER TWELVE

Tuesday morning

I stepped out onto my tiny patio and looked up into the clear dawn sky. It promised to be a glorious morning, which made the tragic events of last night seem doubly unreal. I sighed, hungover from a mostly sleepless night. I couldn't get the picture of CeCe writhing in pain out of my head. I probably never would.

I'd tried to convince myself that her death had been an accident, that her almond milk drink had turned rancid, or that she'd nibbled on some toxic leaf or something else ridiculous, anything except what I knew in my heart was true. That someone had killed her. Deliberately. Those drinks had our names on them, after all. But why would someone here have killed her? And could I be a target?

I heard the rustle of leaves and whipped around. A bird. I felt panicked, but foolish. In turning, I noticed a folded note thumbtacked to the door. Anxiety about my mother having had a heart attack receded as I read, "23:00. Nora Franke please call 'MetroScene' with urgency."

MetroScene? At eleven last night? That's two a.m., New York time. Why on earth . . . Oh, of course. The news must have broken by then. That someone—two someones—had died at a well-known health spa. What a treat for the tabloids, much less for a weekly magazine that thrived on gossip and scandal among the fashionables. "Our reporter, right on the scene, witness to a murder, can't wait to tell you all about it."

I scrunched the note in my fist, furious at the imposition of work on my personal time, then stood on the patio. The more I thought about it, the more I realized it might not be such a bad idea if they wanted me to put on a journalist's cap. It would give me a role, since the police had made it clear as I left the lodge last night that I'd have to stay on here. At least for a while. It would let me work through some of this sadness I felt. Sadness and, yes, anger at CeCe's ugly death. And, less admirably, anger at my own plans being put in disarray.

Maybe I'd be able to think about something other than eating, my usual refuge in times of stress. Only the fact that my tiny refrigerator held just a peach and some raw carrots had prevented a full-scale binge last night. I did think briefly about raiding the spa kitchen, but it was too scary to think about walking alone through the ranch at midnight on that particular night. Even the sounds of the cicadas frightened me.

I stuffed the note in the pocket of my warm-up suit and walked down the hill toward the phone booths. The one outdoor phone on the path didn't get activated until midday, and it was just six ten a.m. Although after nine a.m., hardly anyone would be in the New York office yet—magazine editors, except on closing days, kept what used to be called bankers' hours, arriving at ten a.m. or later. But Danny—Mr. Daniel Thomas McCormick Jr., "managing editor to the stars"—would be there. He was always there. And it was probably he who had made the late night phone call to me anyway.

The lines snaking outside the ranch's only four phone booths were dismaying, and voices could be heard even from the path. Until this morning, I had thought the scarcity of phones and lack of television, radios, even newspapers freeing and refreshing. Now I wanted to scream. All these people calling travel agents, airlines, and car rental offices, making arrangements for when they'd be permitted to leave. I could hear them all too clearly. Even if I had the patience to wait here for a free phone, it would mean broadcasting my plans to the whole ranch. No good. My business was my own business.

Oh, for a working cell phone. But as I'd discovered when I arrived, my stateside phone didn't work here south of the border, and signals across the mountains of Mexico were unreliable anyway.

I headed for the manager's office, but to my further frustration, the little administration cottage was dark. How could it not be open! Surely a morning such as this—even as early as it was—warranted action of major proportions. Phones should be ringing; police hovering; press pressing; staff, guests, families of guests hysterical. Where was everyone? I wanted to jump up and down and howl.

No doubt about it, I had a bad case of what my mother called *shpilkes*—restless bones—an Old World version of high anxiety. There was no way I'd be able to wait on that line for a phone, or hang around until someone showed up at the office. And even when the office opened, it was unlikely they'd let me settle in to use a phone privately. If I couldn't eat chocolate or unload to my friend Judith, I needed to get rid of some of my angst another way.

Switching directions yet again, I made for the meadow where the various hikes assembled. A fast aerobic walk might clear my mind and rid me of some of my excess energy, and I'd still have time afterward to figure out how to call New York with privacy.

There were only a dozen or so hikers at the meadow, with none of the cheerful babble of previous mornings. Those who were there were stretching in silence and standing close together. I spotted Phoebe huddled with her instructor friend, Joe, and kept my distance from them. This was not the morning for Phoebe's brand of brittleness.

After only a few minutes of warm-up, Joe raised his voice and announced that he'd be leading the moderate three-mile meadow hike, setting out at once through the foothills of the mountain.

Never a particularly fast walker, I was some distance from him to begin with, and so had to scurry to catch up. To my surprise, Phoebe, usually a vocal champion of the mountain hike, was in the pack following Joe. At the first bend in the trail, she must have noticed me huffing up behind, because she slowed her pace to let me catch up.

"When they let us leave, will you go?" she asked.

I shook my head. "For the moment, I'm staying put. Assuming the management will want me to. And you?"

Phoebe didn't answer at once, then said, "I could be helpful here. They can use some advice."

"Don't they have a PR agency?" I asked.

"Well of course they do," she snapped. "But I'm sure they're not used to handling hard news. There'll be press and video interest, requests for interviews, travel agents calling. I'm going to speak to Dolores later about how to handle stuff."

She'll probably angle for a fee, I thought. But then, won't I?

As if reading my mind, Phoebe asked, "Are you planning to write about this?"

"It's hardly my line."

"That's hardly a direct answer," said Phoebe.

"Why so anxious about me? Are you planning to write an article?"

"Certainly not. And I'm not anxious. But aside from the . . . distastefulness . . . of taking advantage of a tragedy, I think the less publicity for the ranch, the better."

Phoebe had picked up the pace of our walking. I managed, just, to keep abreast of her.

"You astonish me," I said, gasping for breath. "I thought in your profession, there's no such thing as too little publicity. As long as they spell the name right." This got no response. "Anyhow, in the event that I do write about CeCe and Alan and the ranch, surely it would be from a more sympathetic point of view than an outsider might take."

Whether by design or because of her longer stride, Phoebe soon pulled several feet ahead. This time, I did not attempt to catch up. On other morning walks, the legendary endorphins had kicked in and I would savor the clean, fresh early morning air and the sensation of power my fast walking gave me. Today it felt as if I were pushing through bread dough.

No one else seemed to be enjoying it either. The faces of the women chugging up the trail behind me were guarded, if not grim. They must have realized that if CeCe had not died of food poisoning, and that would be bad enough, someone here—maybe right here—was responsible for her death. Did I really want to be around when they found out who was responsible? It might be—probably was—someone I knew. And maybe liked.

Ahead of me, now climbing one of the steeper inclines on the walk, Phoebe, I could see, had caught up with Joe. They seemed engrossed in conversation. Or at least Phoebe was talking and Joe was listening. I did not like the fact that Joe looked back at me from time to time. Did they suspect me? Of what? Of suspecting them? Could they be planning to get rid of me?

I had always thought that at times of crisis, your heart begins racing like mad. Now, finally grasping the possible risks to myself, I felt as if my legs were made of lead and everything were in slow motion.

The rest of the walk passed in a daze. I was aware of the terrain, more or less. A few times, I stumbled in deep ruts in the road or tripped over rocks I had simply not noticed. Suddenly the questions had ceased to be hypothetical, the anxiety no longer remote. I was irritated with my anxiety but it seemed authentic, as opposed to the angst I'd been living with forever about my weight and my appearance, not to mention my health. Maybe this would get me unstuck. Maybe I could use this nightmare to change my life. Maybe.

As I swung around the final approach to the ranch, I saw Joe and Phoebe standing in the middle of the path. Joe was stretching his calf muscles. Phoebe was still talking.

Phoebe started off in the direction of the dining room, then called back to Joe. "Pick up some of the number fifteen lotion in town, okay?"

Joe didn't answer, but nodded and started to walk toward the administration building.

"Joe, wait up!" I cried on an impulse. I ran after him. "If you're getting a ride into town this morning, can I come along?"

I was not used to talking to people as unresponsive as Joe, and I rushed to fill the silence.

"I need to make some phone calls and I know it will be easier at the border."

Joe finally said, "We're leaving from the lower parking lot after breakfast. Eight thirty." He nodded at me and took off.

I'd had more gracious invitations in my life, but hey, I'd take what I could get. Unless I got more than I counted on. But this couldn't be dangerous. I was sure he was getting a ride with the ranch van, and there'd probably be others going along. I'd run in for my morning drink, take a quick shower, and still have time to meet him.

Morning drink? Was I truly crazy? On the bulletin board outside the lodge was a handwritten notice that the liquid fast program was suspended until further notice. Why hadn't I realized that? Talk about creative blocking. Tea, that was the answer. In my room. Perhaps I'd find a Krispy Kreme in town for breakfast.

CHAPTER THIRTEEN

Tuesday morning

By the time I had had some brisk apple blossom tea, and had showered and changed, I was obliged to run down the hill toward the parking lot to make it on time. Standing squarely in my path was the ranch manager.

Dolores Estrada was a formidable woman: tall, with lustrous black hair pulled back in a taut bun. Her makeup was more obvious than that of most of the women guests, but it suited her vivid coloring and clothes. When I had first met Dolores, I had thought her heavy. Later, I realized it was because she had such large breasts. She was actually fairly slender, but the combination of her height, coloring, and ironclad bosom gave an impression of mass and substance. She exuded efficiency, along with a heady kind of sensuality. A wild combination, not particularly to my taste. But clearly, to somebody's: Dolores had the complacent air of a well-stroked cat.

"I hope you got your message this morning, Ms. Franke," she said. "The phone call was a bit late for us, but one of the boys ran it over to your casita."

Dolores had persisted in calling me "Ms. Franke," thus making it clear we were not buddies and that she harbored no warmth for me or for my role at the ranch. I smiled as sweetly as I could while shifting on my toes so I could take off again.

"I do appreciate it. Thank him for me."

"No bad news, I hope?"

I shook my head, still smiling. You know perfectly well what the message said, you witch. I bet you read all the mail too.

"I must run," I said aloud, attempting to sidestep Dolores on the path.

"Where are you off to so early? Surely this is not the direction of the kitchen. We can't have you playing hooky, now."

Dolores's attempt at playfulness fell dreadfully flat.

"Be back shortly," I said. "And I have a very full afternoon of classes and demonstrations planned. I promise you."

This time, I didn't try to get past her but started running across the dense ground covering of ice plants, crunching them as I ran. By the time I raced down the wide steps to the parking lot I was totally out of breath. I was slightly more fit than when I had arrived, but the extra thirty or so pounds I carried on my small frame really slowed me down. By now the parking lot was crowded with police cars and again taxis from Almagro, even some from San Diego. I realized that several of the guests were arguing with the police, who appeared to be refusing to let them leave in the taxis or in their own cars. *"Mañana,"* they kept saying. "Tomorrow. Maybe tomorrow."

I saw one of the policemen who had questioned me last night. It was easy to recognize him, since he had an enormous mustache that made him look like he was in the cast of *Viva Zapata!* It took a lot of pleading and a short but thoroughly embarrassing pat-down of my body, but after conferring with Inspector Nuñez, he finally agreed that I could go to town for two hours.

Just as I won my victory, the ranch van began to pull away. I called out to Joe in the passenger seat, but he didn't appear to hear me. I started waving my hands frantically and caught the attention of the young Mexican boy driving the van. He slammed on the brakes and reversed, stopping close to where I waited panting.

"*Muchas gracias, amigo,*" I said in my halting Spanish, and asked Joe, "Why didn't you wait for me? You could see me running after you."

"Sorry."

Joe sat staring straight ahead, as silent and remote as always. Then, suddenly, he turned to where I sat behind him and to my astonishment, ignited.

"Phoebe tells me you're a magazine writer, Nora," he said, his eyes intent upon my face. "Must be real interesting."

I think you're trying too hard, Joe. You've ignored me for ten days.

"I just write food articles, restaurant reviews, stuff like that."

"Sounds very exciting," he said, his gaze still glued to my face. "Is that why you're going to the border?" he continued. "To call your magazine?"

I smiled. That little note might as well have been broadcast over the public address system.

"And you?" I asked, sidestepping the question. "What're you doing in town so early in the morning?"

Joe continued to look at me. He doesn't blink, I realized.

"Oh," he murmured, "just need to do a thing or two."

And as suddenly as he had ignited, the flame went out. Poof. Back to dead space.

We rode in silence to the plaza in the center of town, where Joe hopped out of the van without a backward glance. He disappeared into the crowd of young Mexican men milling around the entrance to the small park. Turning to make a mental note of where the taxi stand was alongside the plaza, I noticed my mustachioed policeman behind the wheel of a dark, unmarked car, creeping along behind us. Okay, I thought, they're not so dumb and trusting. I asked the driver to drop me off at the bank of phone booths near the border. Last week, I'd been able to simply walk across the border to the American phone booths. I knew now I'd be forbidden to step across the line.

There was a lineup of cars and vans going the other way, into Mexico. Some of them looked like camera trucks. Probably San Diego news crews. Hadn't I thought—a hundred years ago, yesterday afternoon—that the ranch was a haven of peace and tranquillity?

CHAPTER FOURTEEN

Tuesday midmorning

It felt strange leaving the cocoon of the ranch, however unsafe
that cocoon might presently feel. It was so ugly here. And noisy
and smelly too, after the quiet austerity of my casita. I felt as-
saulted by the grinding gears of the trucks and the cacophony
of car horns. Just as invasive were the smells: tacos being fried
in hot oil, the familiar urban smell of greasy hamburgers and
french fries. I fought off a slight nausea and slipped into one of
the enclosed phone booths to place my call. Thank heavens for
a Mexican phone card.

The conversation with Danny went just as I expected. He
was light and funny and flattering, and agreed to speak to my
agent, Judith, about a fee. He pressed hard for a blockbuster
three-thousand-word news-breaking article by Thursday night. I
convinced him that newspapers and television managed news-
breaking events far better than weekly magazines did, but that
I'd deliver a two thousand- to twenty-five-hundred-word first-
person piece by Friday night at the latest. Fortunately, I had my
point-and-shoot camera with me, and I could probably get some
publicity stills of the ranch from Dolores. Those I would send
on right away. He also agreed that to speed my research along, I
could fax a list of the main players to Wendy, one of the research
assistants. She'd see what she could find out about them. I was
relieved. And I knew there was a fax machine in the reservations office.

While Danny was in such a benevolent mood, I asked for background files on Rancho de las Flores. Before I accepted this job, I had checked out the research library, or morgue, for material about the financing and reputation of the ranch, but now it was time to look closer. Could CeCe—maybe even Alan—have died as part of a plan to ruin the ranch?

I felt better after my conversation with Daniel, alive, energized, and comfortable wearing my reporter's hat again. This might be my chance to prove to Danny (and Max and my mother and my agent and, by the way, myself) that I can do more hard-hitting, investigative writing. Not just fluff, as Max has described my food columns. And of course, although I'd been blocking out the unhappiness, I'd become fond of CeCe in such a short time. She deserved my concern and my efforts to help find the truth.

On impulse, I punched in the familiar number of Max's office. It's true that we were officially on break from each other. After a tortuous summer, during which we had told ourselves it was okay to go out with other people (I had lied), Max had taken me for drinks at the Four Seasons to announce that "our moment had passed." I guess he'd bought the cliché that a woman wouldn't make a scene at such an elegant restaurant, and one at which I was known. He was wrong.

Neither of us was prepared for my reaction when he tried to break up with me, and we finally had to leave when I ran out of tissues and cocktail napkins. I told him he was making the biggest mistake of his (not to mention my) life, and hours later, after more passionate talk and lovemaking than we'd shared in months, we agreed to take a breather. We'd reassess our relationship when I returned to New York.

We hadn't been in touch. In fact, I hadn't told him exactly where I was going. But this was a bit special. After all, he was an experienced U.S. Attorney, head of the Major Crime Unit in the feverishly busy Southern District of New York office of the U.S. Attorney General, and he could be of great help to me. If he so chose.

While I waited for his secretary to find Max, I threw open the door to the phone booth and with my free hand rummaged clumsily through my tote bag for something, anything, to use as a fan. My menu plan for the week would have to do. I felt as if I couldn't breathe. It was undoubtedly the heat beginning to build up in the closed booth. Sure.

"Nora? Are you calling from Mexico?"

"Don't shout, Max. I can hear you fine. How did you know where I was?"

"Rose called me this morning. She got crazed when the story broke about the deaths at your fat farm. You okay?"

I let the "fat farm" comment pass. I had other, more familiar grounds for irritation.

"Does my mother report to you regularly?" I asked.

"Hey, easy. Rose and I understand each other. At least as well as you and I do. Or did." He paused. I let the silence deepen. "I assume you're heading home soon as they let you . . ."

"You assume wrong. I'm staying. And I'm writing an article about it for *MetroScene*. I thought I was calling for moral support."

"Nora, Nora." Max's voice was as measured and deliberate as ever. Despite his inflammatory remarks, I was so damned glad to hear that voice! I could just picture him leaning back in his oversized leather desk chair, calmly puffing at his politically incorrect pipe.

"Why don't you leave all this to the pros, honey?" Puff puff. "You're in Baja California, not San Salvador. They won't railroad people or manufacture evidence. Enjoy yourself. Make friends. Lose that weight you're always obsessing about."

Of course, I rose to the teasing bait.

"Screw you, Max. I have made friends. I am losing weight. Not that it's any of your business. And . . ." My voice rose precipitously. ". . . I know what I'm doing. I am not some little chicklet you met at a singles bar."

"Nora."

I could almost hear the snap of his chair as he sat upright.

"Sniffing out a murderer is not like identifying the herb in a sauce mignonette . . ."

"The hell it's not. Forget it, Weber. I'll call you if I need bail."

"Wait. Don't hang up on me, dammit. And I don't go to singles bars. Fill me in on what's going on."

I told him about Alan's accident—maybe accident—and CeCe's poisoning.

"I was right beside her, Max. And I was totally useless. I just stood by and watched her die. She was such a love. I'm surprised myself at how affected I am by her death, only knowing her a couple of days. This mess . . . it's important to me to make sense of it. I mean, it's really important. I don't know why. This place has gotten to me. I don't want it to go under. And not just because it's working for me." To my surprise, my voice shook. Damn. I'd been fine until I spoke to him.

"You've always got to believe passionately in whatever it is you're doing, honey." Max sounded calmer. "If you've picked it and it's great, then you're great. Validates you. Too bad you don't feel that way about us."

"Are you seeing a shrink?"

"I don't like to think of you in this mess. Come on back to New York. I'll pick you up at the airport . . ."

"You know, I just thought of how you can help me. The local guy in charge of the case—I think he's based in Tijuana—is Inspector Enrique Nuñez. He's very enigmatic—more like my fantasies of a phlegmatic British inspector. He won't even say if it was food poisoning or some other kind of poisoning. Of course, maybe he doesn't know yet. But it would sure help if he knew I didn't have a history as a serial killer, and that I had the confidence of a U.S. Attorney."

"I'll give his office a call." I heard resignation in his voice.

"Fantastic. Oh yeah, it would also help to know something about the ranch . . . Is it up for sale, who really owns it, is their credit good, any trouble with the law?"

"Got it."

Silence again.

I cleared my throat. "Listen, it's going be too hard to reach me at the ranch by phone. And a fax might be too public. I'll call you from a safe phone early tomorrow morning and tell your secretary where and when to fax the info."

"Will you use a code name?"

I laughed, despite myself. "Thanks, Max. I really do appreciate your help. Truly. And I want you to know I've been doing a lot of thinking. About myself. Us."

"Nora . . ."

I hung up quickly, before Max had a chance to say (or not say) how he felt about our being apart. I wasn't really prepared to know.

As I left the phone booth, I noticed the adjacent American-style supermarket. I couldn't resist. I wandered around the store for ten minutes, trying to decide on what it was I wanted.

A Snickers bar? Cheese popcorn? I could see cheating with a buttery croissant or a chewy toasted onion bagel slathered with cream cheese. Maybe an apricot soufflé. Barring those, I might as well get back to midmorning carrot sticks.

CHAPTER FIFTEEN

Tuesday afternoon

The secluded patio was crowded. Clearly I wasn't the only one who wanted to get away from the chaos the serene ranch had become: perspiring policemen trying not to ogle the scantily clad women wandering around the grounds; those very same women whirling around nervously as footsteps sounded on the gravelly paths; women and men who hesitated at the refreshing ice-cold lemonade containers on the dining room terrace before risking a cup. The few men guests at the ranch looked almost apologetic, "It wasn't me" written all over their faces. Lunch had been quick and quiet, attended for sustenance rather than companionship. A note on the bulletin board had advised guests—and me—that the cooking demonstrations and menu talks for the day had been suspended. All would return to normal tomorrow. What was normal anymore? Could they really think CeCe's death would be forgotten that quickly?

I had come here, to this oasis of sunbathing calm behind the women's locker room, to be alone with my thoughts, and was becoming increasingly irritated by the sound of whispers behind me, like mosquitoes buzzing in my ear. I heard Alan's name, then CeCe's. Well, sure. That was inevitable.

I tried to ignore the voices. I didn't need other women's takes on who did what to whom. Suddenly, in the midst of the hushed voices, I heard Simon's name, followed by that of Dolores, followed by snickers. Simon and Dolores? Why was I not really surprised? Hadn't it crossed my mind more than once that Simon and Jody were an incongruous pair? But luscious, full-bodied Dolores? With that tight ass?

I raised the backrest of the chaise to an upright position, adjusted the towel that partially covered my bathing suit–clad body (why couldn't they supply bigger towels?), and took a pad and pencil from my tote. Time to give some thought to my article. Should it be personal—include my own experiences here? Should I name real names? I'd have to call the lawyers at *MetroScene*. Easy enough to write about the ranch, its ambience, its effect on me. Even about Alan and CeCe—and their effect on me. But could I leave it at that? I knew I couldn't—that it would be only a partial story without some theories, suppositions, even guesses as to what had happened and why.

Why not rethink the deaths in light of what I now knew, or at least suspected? Just because some skinny blonde on a chaise lounge coupled their names didn't mean Dolores and Simon were lovers. But it seemed to fit. I'd have to ask around, maybe even interview them. When could they get to spend time together, anyhow? What if—a big list of "what ifs"—what if Simon was frantic to keep the affair from Jody? She adores him, and he adores her money.

Now how do you know that, Franke? I curled up as comfortably as I could on the chaise. This was the part of writing I loved best—playing "what if," arguing with myself, throwing balloons up in the air and popping them. I was leaving out getting the facts; first I had to decide what facts I needed.

I just know Simon adores money, I decided. Think of those cashmere sweaters, the ones that match his eyes. The designer sweats, the trips to Petit St. Vincent he oh-so-casually mentioned. And he drives a silver Porsche. Jody told me so herself. Maybe, I mused, Alan had found out about Dolores. Maybe Simon pushed Alan—no, he couldn't have. Jody would have known he was up on the mountain with Alan. Or would she have?

Was this all just game playing? Could I really be thinking that one of the charming, sophisticated people who had (for the most part) befriended me was capable of murder? Maybe Alan's death was accidental, and someone sought to capitalize on it by killing CeCe. Or maybe it was CeCe who was the danger to the unknown person. What if it was the ranch that was being discredited for some yet-unknown financial reason?

I might have a greater chance of figuring out the answers than that unhappy-looking inspector who had questioned me so severely last night. Who would most likely be his suspects? Certainly the group closest to Alan, and to CeCe as well. Maybe even me, although once he learned I'd never met Alan, and had met CeCe for the first time on Saturday, he'd lost interest. I would add Dolores to my list; it was possible the inspector didn't have her on his.

I was hot and fidgety. I shoved my belongings into my tote and made a quick, self-conscious exit from the patio. Thank heavens the locker room was empty; I'd had all I could take of taut slender bodies. I showered and changed in a leisurely fashion, mulling over all the events of the past few days. By the time I left the spa building, the power of the sun had begun to diminish, and there was even the beginning of a chill in the air. I paused on the path to pull on my windbreaker and glanced over at the administration cottage. The lights in Dolores's office were on, and I decided to drop in without notice.

There was no one in the outer office, but Dolores's door was slightly ajar. I knocked a few times before I heard, *"Quién es?"*

"Nora Franke. I just need a moment."

I didn't wait for a response but sailed on in, sitting down quickly in a chair across the desk from Dolores.

"I've been asked by *MetroScene Magazine* to do a story on the tragedies this week, and I wanted to be sure to represent the ranch as you and the owners would like. So I thought I'd get to you quickly."

I pulled my notebook and pen out of my tote, smiling at Dolores in a matter-of-fact, friendly fashion.

Dolores didn't respond at all. She sat motionless behind her ornately carved wooden desk, looking like a lush, overripe orchid. She smells like one, too, I thought, as I sat with my pencil poised.

"Dolores Estrada, right? E-s-t-r-a-d-a? How long have you been manager here, Dolores?"

"I cannot answer any of your questions. The police do not want me to speak to anyone. I have to discuss the situation with the owners of the resort, first of all things. Phoebe Hollis can give you any information you need."

"Oh no, Dolores, that won't work for me. I only quote direct sources, not flacks. I can get this stuff elsewhere, of course, but I thought you'd welcome an opportunity to make a statement on behalf of Rancho de las Flores."

"I will tell you only this about myself. I was born in Almagro and attended Northern Baja University. I started to work here after graduation and have been a manager for four years. I am very successful here. We hardly lose staff; we always are building and adding facilities. Very few guests have any complaints. This was an unfortunate accident—two accidents. Very tragic. And now, I am going home to sleep before dinner. It has been a very long and difficult day."

"I'm sure it has," I said in my most soothing voice. "You live here at the ranch, don't you?"

Dolores nodded.

"In one of those beautiful villas on the hillside?" I continued.

"You are clearly not a businesswoman. Those villas are for

rent to guests—not for the pleasure of the staff. My cottage is across the stream, very near to yours."

"Tell me about the ranch owners, Dolores. I haven't met them. I only spoke to Christian Benedine, their American representative, before I took the job."

She sat staring at me for a long, silent moment, then, leaning heavily on her forearms, pushed herself up and walked around the desk to the bookcase against the wall.

"Here," she said, handing me a thick white leather scrapbook. "You may borrow this. All you will need to know is here. Please return it by the morning."

I stood up, struggling to gather the scrapbook, my tote bag, and my notebook in my arms and to regain control of the non-interview.

"I can understand your concern about the 'accidents,' Dolores, but surely two deaths in a few days must be more than accidents. Perhaps someone wants to destroy the ranch. Or maybe it was actually directed at the victims. Maybe someone really wanted to kill Alan and CeCe. Could be they'd like to ruin you as well. I should tell you that I've heard rumors about you and a guest . . ."

"Good day," said Dolores icily, as she held the door to her office open and brusquely motioned me through. She was not without dignity, I thought with a grudging respect. And I'd been on a garrulous roll.

"*Adiós*. We'll speak again."

"I think not. You may speak to Phoebe. Or not. But I will not speak with you again. As soon as the police allow, you should leave here. I will speak with the owners. You could write this article at home if you must. It would be wiser. And safer."

Dolores collected her suit jacket and handbag, slammed the door to the cottage behind us, locked it, and clicked off in her astonishingly high heels without looking behind her.

CHAPTER SIXTEEN

Tuesday night

Dinner was the disaster I thought it would be. Back at my room late in the afternoon, I had carefully skimmed the ranch scrapbook for a kind of overview, not at all sure what I was looking for but knowing that I wasn't finding it. Lots of pretty pictures, testimonies about how visiting the ranch changed someone's life, even some pretty fair recipes I'd made note of. A bit of history and anecdotes about how the ranch was founded, nearly fifty years before. But nothing about the ranch's present owners, and certainly nothing to give me an idea why two people might have been killed.

I was terrifically hungry but felt somewhat wary of joining Allison and company for dinner. At lunch, I'd been cruelly ignored. I figured if I got to dinner late, I could sit at a table already formed and not place them and me in an embarrassing position. And so naturally, when I hesitated in the doorway to the dining room, my eyes went straight to the large round table in the rear. Allison was there, and so were a few others of the group, but the empty seats—Alan and CeCe's forever-empty seats—seemed to dominate the whole room. I started when I felt a hand on my shoulder.

"Hey, Nora. You're going to join us, I hope." Tom stood beside me, as friendly and warm as if he hadn't ignored me at lunch. I didn't answer right away. I was captivated by his clear, light blue eyes, the kind Rose would have called WASP eyes. So different from Max's intense black eyes.

Tom didn't wait for me to answer him; he grabbed my hand and pulled me along to the back table. I didn't struggle much. Allison greeted me with seeming delight.

"Nora! Sit yourself down right here." She patted the empty chair beside her. "Unless you're afraid of catching the plague. We're the carriers, incidentally."

I looked around. I hadn't realized until now that the dining room was quieter than usual, and that many—most—of the diners kept looking over at our table. What were they thinking? Two down, six to go?

"I'm sorry we all ignored you at lunchtime, lamb, but CeCe's Buddy was sitting with us and he was hurting so. It didn't seem right to introduce him to a new friend. He was having a hard enough time dealing with all of us old ones."

"He was mean," said Jody, her sharp little face tightening in anger. "Really nasty. Especially to Simon," she added, placing her thin, tanned hand on his. He very carefully extricated his hand, ostensibly to cut his food.

"Buddy had to blame someone, or someones, and we were the most convenient." Phoebe shrugged as if it hadn't bothered her a bit; it might not have.

"Where is he now?" I asked.

"He's moved to a motel, closer to regional police headquarters in Tijuana," said Tom. "He'll be taking her home as soon as they release her body. Hell. I need food." He stood and looked around, finally spotting our waitress and indicating that he and I needed to be served.

"I don't much care that she's dead, and Buddy sensed that. That's why he was so cold to me." Simon spoke dispassionately. "Actually, I don't care about Alan either."

"I can't believe you're saying this," cried Jody, staring at her husband as if she'd never seen him before. "You know how much I loved Alan, and darling CeCe . . ."

"CeCe was very cute, and very rich and, I'm afraid, very foolish. And she talked a lot about things that were none of her business. As for Alan . . . Well, I never liked or trusted him." Simon scraped his chair back from the table. "Excuse me," he said, running his eyes around the table as if assessing his audience. "I'll see you up at the villa, Jode."

No one spoke as Simon strode off, then Jody turned to me.

"It's your fault," she practically spat at me. "Everyone knows you're digging around for dirt and looking for old scandals and stuff."

Phoebe pitched right in.

"I thought we had agreed that I'd handle the press stuff and you'd stay out of it," she said. "You got Dolores all worked up this afternoon . . ."

"I never agreed to stay out of anything, Phoebe." My voice shook with anger. "I'm sure you'll do a great public relations job for the ranch, but I'm a journalist, not a press agent. I have a different job to do. One that's become important to me. And it could benefit the ranch as well."

I put down my fork. Somehow I'd lost interest in the asparagus and tomato soufflé we'd finally been served.

"Good for you." Tom looked approvingly at me. "We've all got to know what happened. Stop pretending that it has nothing to do with us, Phoebe. Jody."

Both women continued to glare at me. Allison stood.

"I could use some fresh air. Take a walk?" she asked me.

I glanced quickly at Tom, and Allison laughed.

"It'll be a short walk. You'll be in the lodge, Tom?"

He caught my eye and smiled, then nodded. Damn, I hadn't thought I'd been that obvious.

Allison and I didn't talk much at first. We walked slowly through the rock garden outside the dining room, then started up the path to the upper villas. It was a sparkling night, the sky clear and star-filled, the air heavy with the scent of honeysuckle. When we got to the top of the hill, Allison veered away from the little paths to the villas and turned into the pool area.

This was my very favorite place at the ranch. The pool was not lap- or Olympic-sized like the one in the fitness area, but free-form, edged partway by Mexican tiles and the rest of the way with brilliantly colored flowering shrubs, some arching gracefully over the edge of the pool. The patio furniture, too, was different from the streamlined vinyl pieces around other pools on the property. Here, the chaises, benches, and chairs had old-fashioned oak frames and thick, luxurious cushions in brilliant colors. The tables were made of stone, the tops inlaid with colorful marble chips. Overhead, the wooden latticework was hung with at least a dozen baskets, tuberous begonias of yellow, pink, orange, and red spilling over in abandonment.

Allison sat down at the edge of a chaise, staring into the moonlit water.

"So," she finally said in a soft, husky voice. "Which one of us did it?"

I sat across from her, on an adjacent bench, and tried to match her cool.

"Well, it wasn't you or Tom. You're my friends. Besides, both of you loved Alan and CeCe."

"Yes, that's true. I did love them." Allison's voice gentled; the words sat heavily in the night air.

"I doubt it was Phoebe. She's too self-absorbed," I continued. "Although her boyfriend Joe's a suspicious one. I caught a ride into Almagro with him this morning. He was very palsy with the guys hanging out in the square, and I bet he knows the border guards, too. Probably floats back and forth at will. Maybe he runs dope, and Alan found out. Then CeCe could have seen something . . ."

"Whoa, there." Allison started to laugh. "An awful lot of maybe's, honey lamb. Although I'm perfectly willing to think the worst of Pal Joey." She smiled sadly. "That's what CeCe called him."

"Then there's Simon. I don't like him, either. Handsome and smooth he may be, but there's something scuzzy about him. He doesn't seem to care much about Jody. At least he's not very nice to her in public. And rumor has it that he and Dolores are screwing around."

"Tsk, tsk. Listening to rumors, are you?" I noticed she didn't confirm or deny them. "Any 'bout me?"

"No one's talked about you in front of me, Allison. But then, everyone must know we're friends. Tell me, what would they say?"

I was teasing, but Allison didn't smile. I had lost her again, her eyes going back to the glowing water in the pool. I suddenly remembered how proprietary Allison had been toward Simon the first time I met him. She had touched him with affection and intimacy, drawing back as soon as Jody joined us. But then, I also recalled CeCe saying something about Allison having had lunch or dinner with Alan in San Diego, and that Alan's brothers-in-law didn't much like it. But Allison was so much older than Alan, wasn't she? And she seemed so much more worldly than the Alan I'd heard about. And much nicer than the Simon I'd gotten to know. Curiously, while she was certainly attractive and sensual, I couldn't really visualize her with either man.

We continued to talk quietly, in a desultory manner, about Alan and his wife, Mariana, as well as CeCe and her husband. Allison seemed more vulnerable than I'd yet seen her. Sadder, too. Finally, I began to get restless.

"I'm heading down the hill, Allison. You be all right here?"

"Bedtime for me, Nora. See you in the morning. Thanks for

being such a good listener."

I hugged her impulsively and left her sitting by the pool. It was only then that I realized I wasn't such a good listener; she hadn't said very much about herself at all.

It took me a few minutes to find the path to the lodge; the ground-hugging lights were pretty but threw off little illumination. Clouds had dimmed the bright moonlight, and there were shadows on the ground. The unevenness of the stepping-stones forced me to walk slowly. I wasn't thrilled to be walking alone in the near dark. I had tried all day to ignore the group hysteria around me but wondered at my flirting with danger out here. Did I not really believe in the danger? Did I think myself immune?

I tried to concentrate on tomorrow: time to go on the offensive. I wanted—needed—this story to be good, to show my editors that I could write hard copy. To get my name out there. And maybe, just maybe, we'd all see that I was more than just a food writer.

I needed to speak to Christian, the ranch's representative in San Diego. I'd call him first thing in the morning. Then there were Mariana's brothers: they were right here at the ranch and should have some info about Alan and . . .

That was the last thing I remember before I hit the ground.

CHAPTER SEVENTEEN

Wednesday afternoon

It was Tom who had spotted me on my way down the hill around nine thirty last night. It had taken me a while to gather my wits about me and push myself to my feet. I hadn't lost consciousness but felt nauseous from the shock and shaky from the pain (my left knee hurt like hell and my right pinkie was weirdly distorted). I was also terrified.

Tom had finally given up waiting for me in the lodge and was making his way up the path to his hacienda when, as he described to me later, he saw an apparition. There was this ghostlike figure weaving from side to side on the path, one arm elevated high above her head. Sounds of sobbing added to the otherworldliness of the scene. Once he recognized me and saw the misshapen finger on my elevated hand, he thought I was crying from pain, but the pain wasn't really that bad. I was so scared. Some brave investigative reporter I turned out to be. Someone must have been on the path behind me when I'd left Allison. Maybe after listening to our conversation. I was sure I hadn't tripped over a rock or the uneven ground but had been purposely pushed. I could feel the pressure of a hand against my back even now. The pain in my knee and finger delivered a clear message: back off.

It turned out my pinkie had been dislocated, not broken, when I had tried to break my fall with my hands. The good doctor yanked it back into place without giving me so much as a shot of Novocain, and I almost passed out from that pain. I didn't object to the overly long splint the doctor shaped: it helped me to remember this was not an intellectual exercise. For some bizarre reason, I wasn't going to say anything about having been pushed. Let everyone think I was clumsy.

Tom was terrific. He took me home and waited until I swallowed my pain pills. Nice man. And maybe there was an attraction. Okay, a real strong attraction. I'd been having fun fantasizing about him and flirting with flirting. But the one I really wanted was Max.

I thought about Max as I lay on the massage table. We'd never actually lived together, except on vacation—our approaches to life are so different. But he makes me laugh and constantly surprises me. Beneath the calm, pragmatic surface is a touch of the poet: he's sensitive to beautiful writing, compassionate about people, and committed to social justice as well as to the Knicks.

We don't share everything, of course. Given my blossoming reputation as an offbeat food critic and writer, it's tough that he's a conservative and picky eater, thinking Chinese and Italian food the only ethnic fare worth considering. Most regrettably and painfully for both of us, he really likes thin women. Not slender, thin. How did we hook up? Even at my thinnest, he'd pinch my midriff or watch what I'd eat. Now . . . he's turned off. And while I'm miserable about it, I'm also mad as hell. I'll show him. I'll get really fat.

Of course, I can't picture my life without him.

No way, of course, would I tell him or my mother about my "accident." Rose would fly down instantly—no plane necessary—and insist that she take me home. Max wouldn't come himself—too busy—but he'd arrange transportation for me. And send flowers with the driver. But I wasn't about to leave. I'd have to do without their sympathy. I could, of course, tell

Judith. Ever since college, when we'd regularly comforted each other after a disastrous date, or cleaned up after each other when one of us had had too much to drink, we'd been true. Judith would commiserate and worry a lot, but she'd assume I was staying. A deal being a deal. But it was more than that. This was my shot at being taken seriously.

As soon as the reservation office opened this morning, I checked and found the fax from *MetroScene*. I had walked there as fast as I could, hoping I could collect the fax before too many people had read it.

It was going to take more than a skim to absorb all the financials on the ranch and the pages of notes my assistant, Wendy, had sent about the cast of characters. She had worked fast. I tucked the papers away in my tote bag, trying not to jar my splinted finger. I borrowed one of the phones in the office and tried to call Christian in the San Diego office of the ranch. He wasn't in, but I left a message on his voice mail saying it was urgent that we speak. Then I called Max and told his secretary, Alice (who pretended not to recognize my voice, or to know anything about why I was calling), that I'd wait at this fax machine between two thirty and three this afternoon. Mexico time.

My last call was to Alan's wife—widow—in La Jolla, but Mariana was just leaving for police headquarters north of here, and had no intention of stopping at the ranch. She did reluctantly agree to a phone interview tomorrow afternoon and said she'd ask her brothers here at the ranch to see me. She warned me that they had minds of their own and might very well decide not to.

Feeling virtuous about checking off most of this morning's to-do list, I spent a couple of hours with the chef, soothing Miguel's ruffled ego; he still felt threatened by my presence here. South or north of the border, chefs are convinced they are unique, creative, and misunderstood. Actually, so are food consultants. We flattered each other, flirted a bit, tasted a few new additions to the menu, and left each other smiling and reasonably content.

To top off my morning, I curled up in an oversized club chair in the lodge. I'd decided it would be wise to stay within sight and sound of others. It was spookily quiet around the ranch. No one had been permitted to leave yet, and guests appeared to be sticking close to their casitas. I managed to absorb most of the information I'd received earlier from *MetroScene*. The ownership of the ranch was a stunner: the mystery partners of Rancho de las Flores Ltd. were Carlos Tamayo and Partners, based in Tijuana, and, surprise! The "Partners" turned out to be the Cerillo boys, Mariana's still-unseen brothers. They of the acres of marijuana fields at the base of the mountain. Were they playing both sides of the twenty-first century's "feel-good" spectrum? Caring for pale, white northern bodies with holistic nurturing while selling pot and who knows what else as a more cynical, and probably more profitable, sideline? Maybe it was they who'd warned me off, not wanting me to dig into Alan and CeCe's deaths? But in truth, all they needed to do was fire me; *MetroScene* sure wouldn't pay me to stay on here, and I couldn't afford it on my own.

Maybe they weren't all in this together. After all, I had been hired to add excitement and modernity to the pure, simplistic menu and to produce a big, beautifully illustrated cookbook that would be a great advertisement for the ranch. That's a rather sophisticated plan for what I had understood to be a family of local gardeners.

What if they decided to abandon the whole project? What if they abandoned me? I'd definitely been ready for a massage; hell, I was ready for a margarita. I was achy and sore. My forehead hurt where I had bumped it. My finger hurt. Even my knees, where I'd fallen, hurt.

The massage had been spectacular . . . it could have lasted twice as long. And so here I was, in a dark, aromatic wrap room, waiting to be wrapped.

Allison and a suddenly solicitous Jody had practically shoved me in here after lunch, telling Elena, the sweetly smiling, chunky attendant, to give me something called an herbal wrap. Allison promised it would "release all the bad toxins in my body" and leave me relaxed and refreshed. Not to mention thinner, from loss of fluids. Well, I wasn't counting on the thinner part. I'd heard that promise all too often throughout my life, but even just lying here waiting for the wraps I could feel myself relaxing.

"*Señorita* Nora, I am ready for you now."

Elena spoke so softly I could barely hear her over the New Agey music in the background.

"These sheets, they are linen, soaked in hot oils and herbs. Very beautiful way to draw out the bad fluids in your body, and to make your skin very soft."

She spoke slowly and carefully; she must have to repeat this explanation several times a day. I was relaxed after the massage and getting sleepy in the warm room. It was initially a shock to feel the steaming-hot, fragrant sheets wrap around my legs, but I accommodated myself to the moisture and heat pretty rapidly. Elena then slowly continued the wraps up the length of my body. I was nervous about the sheets confining my arms, and sensitive hand, as she wrapped them to my sides, but tried to dismiss my discomfort. Hell, nearly everyone I'd met here talked about how soft and clean their skin was after an herbal wrap; how rejuvenated they felt.

What I started to feel as the hot treated sheets began to tighten around my limbs and torso was deep anxiety. By the time Elena tucked my curls into a shower cap, slicked my lips with some sort of pomade, and set cool, wet cotton pads on my eyelids, I'd begun to relax again. I did feel a bit like a sweet-smelling mummy, but didn't even murmur when Elena explained that she was turning up the heat in the room slightly, and I should try to sleep. I heard the door click shut.

I was in the middle of a delicious half dream, in which both Max and Tom were simultaneously stroking my body and commenting on how silky my skin was, when I felt a slight cooling of the air. *Someone's come into the room,* I thought sleepily. Another mummy-to-be. I turned my head, but realized I couldn't get my hands free to remove the pads from my eyes. I didn't like that but tried not to feel too claustrophobic as the wet cloths continued to tighten around my body. It would be over soon, and just think about that silky skin!

Quiet footsteps passed around the foot of the table.

"Elena?" I asked. "Is that you? I think I'd like to be unwrapped now. This is enough for my first time. *Por favor?*"

No one answered, but the muffled footsteps were approaching the head of the table now.

"Who is it?" I tried to sound forceful.

Still no answer.

I didn't like this. In fact, I really hated it. I started to panic. My heart began to race. I used all of the strength I'd been developing in my stomach muscles to pull myself up, but I was wrapped too tight to get my arms loose and I couldn't budge. I felt motion around my face, then my heart practically stopped with terror as a hot, moist cloth descended on my nose and mouth. Pressure. Then nothing.

CHAPTER EIGHTEEN

Wednesday afternoon, continued

Bright, glaring lights. I kept my eyes tightly shut. The room was cold and noisy. Voices, whispering. If I concentrated real hard, my head hurt, but I could make out someone saying, "She's awake." Then a man's voice: "Another few minutes. A different story." Another voice wailed, "No! no!" Was that me?

I shivered, despite the still-warm sheets.

"Easy, lamb. Everything's all right now. You're safe."

Allison. She was stroking my forehead, now lifting my head slightly so I could drink some water. I'd been crying.

"Someone . . ." I began, my voice hoarse and shaky.

"Yes, we know. They've called for the nurse and the police. Can't imagine what's keeping them. There're enough of them around. Poor Elena is over in the corner, crying and wringing her hands. And Maria . . . the receptionist, you know? She's running in and out, creating a major fuss. She did help unwind you, though."

Allison's voice trembled, revealing her distress.

"How? Who found me?" I whispered. I tried to sit up but, feeling dizzy and nauseated, fell back on the table. Was that Simon standing close by, looking grim and worried? Jody hovered near him, in the midst of what seemed like a mob scene.

"Jody did. I followed close behind." Allison beamed with pride. Why? Did they save my life? Interrupt someone?

"We wanted to peek in and see how you liked the herbal

97

wrap. Jody was here earlier than me. When she saw that drugged-soaked cloth on your face, she let out such a scream . . ."

It wasn't until Allison said "drug-soaked" that I realized what that sickly-sweet smell was. Ether. Or chloroform? I gagged, then pressed my uninjured hand against my mouth and searched wildly for a container. Jody grabbed a wastebasket for me, and I lost breakfast and lunch, maybe yesterday's dinner too. Memories came flooding back: I remembered my six-year-old terror when I awoke in the tiny private hospital after my tonsils were removed; the acrid taste of vomit in my mouth and roughness in my throat; the loneliness until I saw my father snoozing in an easy chair by the window; the slippery sweetness of vanilla ice cream being spooned into my dry mouth by my unusually solicitous mother.

"I have to get out of here," I whispered to Allison, who nodded in instant understanding and helped me stand up.

"*Señorita,* you must stay." Elena came running over. "The nurse, she is coming. I call Dolores. She is coming too . . ."

I put my hand on Elena's shoulder and told her that I didn't blame her for what had happened to me, but no, I didn't want the nurse. Or Dolores.

"It must have been a joke," I told her. She looked at me as if I were crazy. I didn't care; I had to get out of there.

With Allison and Jody's help, I got to the locker room and managed to rinse out my mouth, wash my face, pull on my shorts and T-shirt, and slip out the back door before anyone official came looking for me. I wasn't ready to answer questions; I wanted to ask them. I needed to ask them. But first I had to pull myself together.

The chilly afternoon air helped to revive me, although I imagined I could still smell the chloroform hanging in the air. Jody fussed a bit, insisting that we find Inspector Nuñez, who was investigating the double "incidents," as she put it. I promised I would speak to him: pigheaded I may be, but not entirely self-destructive.

"Someone wanted to frighten you."

I was startled by Simon, who had silently appeared beside us.

"I figured that out by myself," I retorted sharply.

"I mean, frighten you as opposed to kill you. It would have been easy enough to hold that stuff on your face a few crucial moments longer."

I started to tremble. I couldn't stop. I hugged my shoulders as if that would give me control over my body, but it didn't work.

I could hear someone running around the corner of the building, breathing hard from exertion or emotion.

"Nora! My God, Nora, you could have been killed!"

It was Tom. The tears came to my eyes again.

"I'm okay, Tom. Just a bit . . ."

He didn't ask, just grabbed me and held me very tight. I could feel myself calm. I stopped shaking and let myself be held. He wasn't Max, but he was kind and comforting.

Simon and Jody made noises about appointments and disappeared after I thanked them for helping me.

"I'm beginning to get tired of this."

My throat was sore and a world-class headache had begun to make itself known. "First last night, now this."

"What do you mean last night?" asked Allison. "You fell, lamb. Tripped on a stone, maybe."

"I think I was pushed. I could feel it. I obviously am some sort of threat to somebody. Maybe I know something I don't know I know."

Tom held me away so he could look at me. "Pushed? Are you sure, Nora? You were upset, frightened. Maybe . . ."

"I was pushed." I glared at him. "Almost certainly. And I'm

really pissed."

"He or she must have wanted to warn you off," said Tom slowly.

"Well, it didn't work. And today . . . oh hell, I don't know. Jody could have interrupted whoever just in time, or else the hypothetical he or she just wanted me to be scared again. If so, they should be pleased. I am."

I thought for a moment about what I'd just said.

"It could have been Jody. She's the one who found me. Or could it have been a he?"

"Yeah. There's a door from the men's locker into the wrap room," Allison explained. "The boys have their own massage rooms—not as many as ours, of course. But some of the fellas have been known to get herbal wraps. Especially after a heavy-duty workout. I've seen Simon in there."

"And me," said Tom. "But only once."

Allison walked around a bit, restless and worried.

"Any real sense of who all it could have been? Not Jody. I won't believe it was Jody. Who might have tried to, you know . . ."

"Smother me?" I shook my head. Ouch. That was a mistake.

"But you're feeling all right now? Stronger?"

"Yes." I smiled, or tried to. "I came here to feel better about myself. So I've got bruised knees, a dislocated finger, a major headache, a sore throat, and I'm scared shitless. But I've lost some weight! And I'm not leaving!"

Tom shook his head.

"C'mon Nora. We need to talk to that cop. Maybe he'll help you see reason."

I ignored his comment but used his arm to test my balance. Not too bad. We walked slowly around to the front of the spa building and started up the path to the ranch office. I was feeling stronger, all right, and angry. Bone-deep angry. I didn't like being pushed around, and I thought it was time to push back.

CHAPTER NINETEEN

Later Wednesday afternoon

Ahead of us, at the entrance to Dolores's office, stood a tall, muscular man with a briefcase. He looked like a weight lifter, not too comfortable in his conservative, well-tailored business suit. He looked me over carefully, particularly at my curly black hair, as if making sure I fit a description.

"Ms. Franke?" His voice was deep and modulated. At my nod, he said, "I'm Christian Benedine. We spoke when you took your position here. I got your message that you wanted to see me."

I stepped forward, waving good-bye to Allison and Tom. Allison seemed mildly amused at my abrupt dismissal of her. Tom hesitated but I assured him I knew who Christian was.

"He works for the ranch. In San Diego," I explained. "Sort of a marketing person."

Tom continued to look skeptical; I couldn't blame him. Christian looked more like an enforcer than a businessman.

"Shall we talk in the manager's office?" I asked as we shook hands.

"She's there," he said. "I think we need more privacy."

"I'm expecting a fax just about now, up in the reservations office. Do they have any private space?"

"Follow me."

Christian set off quickly for the ranch offices, placed somewhat apart from the main ranch. I waved good-bye again

101

to Tom, who still didn't look happy about my leaving with this stranger. But this was precisely what I wanted. Christian would be my conduit to the Cerillos.

We didn't speak as he took the hill to the offices in what seemed like only a few bounding steps. I huffed along behind Christian, still feeling shaky and weak. The air had helped, but I stopped at the water fountain outside the building and took my time soothing my throat and settling my queasy stomach. There was no sign of the police; good thing I didn't really need them.

Christian led the way to a small, dark room behind the bank of telephones and the fax machine. I asked the operators to let me know when a fax from the U.S. Attorney's office arrived, and noticed Christian's surprise and, I'd like to think, dismay. I pointed out that it was stuffy in the office, so I casually propped the door open with my tote bag and sat near it, in the visitor's chair. I was not going to take any more unnecessary chances. Christian had already snagged the chair behind the desk anyhow. I couldn't imagine him accepting any other than a dominant role. He clasped his hands in front of him and rested them on the desk.

"I've been asked by the owners of Rancho de las Flores to discuss with you the article you're planning to write for a New York City magazine." Christian started off slowly and ponderously, then picked up speed as he got further along in his spiel. "They are sure you will remember that you are first of all an employee, a temporary employee of course, of the ranch, and your primary loyalty must therefore be to the ranch."

My eyes had glazed over by now. I had been sure this would be the approach they would take.

"Let's cut to the chase, Christian," I said after a few more weighty remarks. "I follow the party line or else get tossed? And what is the party line anyway?"

Christian sat quietly, his hands still folded together and his gaze steady and calm.

"Alan Nardy's death was a tragic accident. He was not a strong hiker, had been warned, as everyone is warned, not to climb the mountain alone, and he died of exposure after falling at night. As I understand it, you never met Mr. Nardy, so you can only write of your acquaintances' reactions to him and to his death. Cecelia Clayton is another matter. I'm told—"

"By Dolores, right?" I interrupted.

"Dolores told me that you and Cecelia had become friends. Even so, of only a few days. It is likely that she told you her theories about Alan Nardy's death. Whatever they might have been. They were very close friends. Possibly more than friends. Possibly she couldn't bear to live after he died . . ."

It hurt my throat, but I started to laugh. His attempt to put a suicide spin on CeCe's death was so absurd that I couldn't restrain myself.

"Christian," I said sweetly, "let's skip right over this suicide thing. You don't even believe it yourself."

I was a bit surprised to see his lips curl slightly in what might pass for a smile in a less robotlike man.

"I think I should tell you," I went on, "that I'm aware of who the owners of the ranch are, so we needn't pussyfoot around their names. Actually, I don't know who Carlos Tamayo is, but I was planning to call on Victor and Romero this afternoon. Maybe you could help me get in touch with them. Mariana suggested it. (Small lie.) I think it's time I met the Cerillo brothers without their farmer disguises."

Christian's gaze held mine. "That should be an interesting meeting," he said.

The words were neutral enough, but I thought his tone of voice mocking. Even mildly threatening. As he picked up the phone, one of the secretaries beckoned to me from the doorway. Max's documents must have come through.

The fax machine was still stuttering as I approached it, the official-looking pages shooting out to form a formidable pile. I started to scoop them up, not wanting anyone but me to see them. They went on forever! Christian was standing in the doorway to the back office, his eyes on the faxed pages. He raised an eyebrow at me.

"Just one more minute," I promised. "Research."

"We now have an appointment with the Cerillos in twenty minutes, Ms. Franke."

"Nora."

"It's not a long walk to where they live, but in light of your recent mishaps we'll take the ranch Jeep."

I glared at Christian. Mishaps. The information system here was remarkable.

The fax machine finally stopped spewing out pages, and I gathered them up, then shoved them unceremoniously into my tote bag, along with the earlier faxed pages. I didn't want Christian to think these were worth hurting me for. If the Cerillos were indeed marketing marijuana and coke, as *MetroScene*'s research had seemed to suggest, they'd need a tough, semisophisticated enforcer. I almost laughed out loud. I was thinking like an Elmore Leonard crime story.

"Where do they live? Mariana's brothers, I mean." I tried to sound ingenuous but had little faith in my ability to mask my nervousness.

"Just outside the ranch property, Ms. Franke."

"Nora. And I've been thinking. Maybe I could ask a friend to come with me . . ."

"I don't think that will be necessary, Ms. Franke. They only want to meet you, and as I said, our appointment is now in ten minutes."

Christian put his hand under my elbow and gently but firmly moved me forward. My curiosity overcame my qualms, and I followed his lead.

"The Cerillos have a small compound, I believe that's what the Kennedy family called their enclave, right? One big house for each brother, then a smaller guesthouse, for when other family members come to visit. And there are a dozen or more cottages for workers. They rent them out to ranch employees, as well as to extended family. I've got a nice one myself. With a garden."

I tried to picture Christian stopping to smell the roses, but the message was clear enough. Victor and Romero Cerillo were surrounded by friends and family, and no one was going to come upon them unexpectedly. This became especially clear after we exited the beautifully intricate wrought-iron gate of the ranch and turned the corner in almost a U-turn. We very shortly passed through another gate, this one serious and manned, and drove at least a mile to a fenced-in, paved parking court. There were several of the omnipresent ranch pickup trucks, another Jeep, and three or four utility vans parked. Inside the handsome triple garage, which looked as if it had once been horse stables, were shiny black cars. My knowledge of cars was limited to Max's 1973 red MGB and an occasional rental Toyota, but even I couldn't mistake the distinctive Mercedes emblems on their hoods.

We parked and walked up a wide, open path bordered by a riotous mixture of yellow marigolds, hot pink ranunculus, red salvias. Like many Mexican houses, the large stone building before us revealed little about itself or its inhabitants. Undoubtedly there was a patio, even a garden or pool, enclosed by an interior courtyard. But as I reached the front door, it opened, and I had a feeling I'd never get to see that patio.

CHAPTER TWENTY

Wednesday, late afternoon

It wasn't as if he was a very large man, or as if he was carrying a weapon (that I could see). He was only four or five inches taller than me. But he looked mean. And cold. Ice-cold. He stood straight, arms akimbo. He was slight, clean-shaven, with longish black hair. He stared at me silently, without blinking, and I stared back. He scared me to death.

Behind me, Christian cleared his throat.

"This is Nora Franke. Ms. Franke, Romero Cerillo."

"Buenos días, Señor."

He nodded his head and motioned us inside. I hoped I wouldn't embarrass myself by throwing up.

We followed him into a cool, tiled foyer, then past a formal sitting room stuffed with heavy carved oak furniture, and a dining room similarly furnished. He led us to a techno-wonderland at the back of the house. The office was clean and spare, yet filled with business toys: a fax machine, copier, two serious-looking computers, two or three complicated-looking phones. Three cellular phones and a number of beepers or pagers sat on the desk. The house was still and quiet; I could just barely hear the murmur of women's voices behind the dining room. Romero motioned us farther on into the office and closed the door behind us. At that point, bravado notwithstanding, my heart started to beat wildly. I swallowed a lot and tried not to look as scared as I felt. Was this dumb of me, or what?

"*Señor* Cerillo," I said firmly. "My sympathy on the loss of your brother-in-law."

He was startled and seemed not to know what to say.

"*Gracias, Señorita,*" came a voice behind me.

Standing in the office doorway was the flip side of Romero: this had to be Victor. They looked remarkably alike, except that Victor was in perpetual motion, smiling, shaking hands, pulling out a chair for me, waving Christian out of the room. I didn't like that. At least Christian was the devil I knew. And he spoke English.

"You do not speak Spanish, I think," commented Victor, as if reading my mind.

"You would think that living in New York, hearing Spanish all the time, I'd have learned it by now, but no. I'm sorry."

Why are we having this ditsy conversation?

"*Señorita* Franke . . . Nora, if I may?"

I nodded.

"Please, I am Victor, as you must guess. You should not look so nervous here. We wish only to speak with you. Your life, you understand, has become strangely linked to ours. My brother's and mine."

Romero, I noticed, took second place to his voluble brother. He sat down at a desk on the far side of the office and leaned back in his chair. Watching.

"Not only have you become a much-valued employee of our ranch," continued Victor, "—yes, your research is quite correct, my congratulations to your magazine and to your lover—but since Cecilia Clayton's death you have become, shall I say, uncomfortably curious about our operations."

"Former lover. And I do know that you and your brother are in partnership with someone named Carlos Tamayo, and you all own Rancho de las Flores. What's the big secret? And which of you actually runs the ranch?"

"Ah, something you do not know. Yet. I'm sure the information is in that big fax you have yet to read. I will tell you. Carlos has a daughter, Ana. She is very beautiful, very brilliant. Her English is *excelente*—she speaks much better than I do. Than any of us. Even Christian." Victor laughed heartily at his joke. Romero did not blink.

I realized now who Ana was. It was she I had spoken to about working at the ranch, she who had handled my contract, welcomed me. But all on the phone.

"I'm not sure I understand," I said. "You and your brother, and this Carlos, Ana's father, own the ranch—for what purpose? It's hard for me to think of you as a fitness aficionado. Or a vegetarian. Is it a cover?"

"A cover? For what, *Señorita?* You make up so much drama. We have ranched this area for many years—cows, hay, wheat. The old owners, the original owners, of the ranch, they were the ones so interested in health. But even they get tired, old, need money. My brother and I ask our friend Carlos to help us buy the ranch from the old people."

Victor stood and began to pace around the room, sweeping his arms around in grand gestures.

"We are proud to do this, you understand. After so many years of ranching for them, for others, it is good to be an owner. And we are proud of Rancho de las Flores. We hire professionals, experts in their fields, to take charge of the different areas. Like yourself," and he nodded his head to me. "Ana is in touch all the time with Dolores. She comes here every month. Our cousin Fredo takes care of the flowers, the landscaping. Another relative makes the engineering—maintenance! That is the word. All of this you can say in your magazine."

"Can I talk about the marijuana fields out yonder, and how much they may have to do with Alan's and CeCe's deaths? About rumors of newer, less amusing ventures into cocaine traffic? And about my 'mishaps,' as Christian described the assaults to my body?"

Victor's eyes skimmed my body as I spoke. I refused to let myself react. I spoke firmly and steadily, although privately I thought I was out of my mind revealing myself so fully and suggesting what I was suggesting. I could hear Romero shift behind me.

Victor started to laugh. In contrast to his brother's quiet, even sinister demeanor, he was turning out to be charming and good-humored. Or was I just naive?

"I'm not laughing at you, Nora, or at these assaults. I laugh at the notion that you could be such a threat to my brother and myself that we would try to harm you. And so clumsily! May I offer you a drink? Tecate beer, perhaps? Sealed?"

I shook my head, wishing it didn't still throb.

"Ah, too bad. Now I cannot properly have one. But you are undoubtedly right. It would bother your head. Your finger? It is less painful, I hope? Dr. Singh told us you were very brave."

I got the message. He knew everything he wanted to know about me.

"Um, Victor. If my magazine and my friend were able to find out all this info about your drug activities, don't you think the law knows as well?"

"What drug activities? Oh it's true, of course, that we once did grow marijuana. But so does everybody down here. Including policemen. They've been here many times, but they have never found any other drugs. And now, you will see when you return, the marijuana is gone."

"Gone? Are you actually saying . . . ?"

"A little crop of marijuana that never existed had nothing to do with Alan or Cecilia Clayton's deaths. I swear it. And by the way, I wouldn't dream of hurting one of your magnificent black curls—and so incompetently, too. No, *Señorita Nora*, you will have to look elsewhere for your murderer. Perhaps closer to home."

Curiously, I believed him.

"How close to home?"

He chuckled, looking pleased with himself.

"I cannot do all of your work for you, Nora. And I am sorry about Alan Nardy. I thought him an idiot of a man, one who talked too much and had too big eyes for other women. But he made my sister happy. And I am very fond of Jorge." At my quizzical look he added, "The baby of my sister and of Alan."

"And CeCe?"

"Ah, her I only saw in passing. Too thin. Too nervous."

My headache was back, maybe as much from what I wasn't learning as from the earlier "mishap." I felt tired and confused. I dismissed what Victor had to say about his "little crop" of marijuana. Those were acres and acres of fields I'd seen. And this house and three Mercedeses, not to mention the ranch, were not the result of small crops of anything. Could a fitness ranch be that lucrative?

My loss of energy must have been apparent, because Victor suddenly ushered me out into the hallway. Before I had even enough time to be frightened, I stepped outside into the courtyard I'd never thought to see. Striped awnings and tall arches covered with climbing roses shaded most of it, and thickly cushioned gliders and chairs filled nearly every square foot. Around the edges of the courtyard were perfect little mini-gardens, with brilliant pink, yellow, and orange ranunculus as well as almost shockingly orange Mexican sunflowers. In the center of the courtyard was a small tiled lily pond. Exquisite.

"Mariel," he called. "Some iced tea, *por favor.*"

I noticed that Romero hadn't followed us out here. Nor was Christian anywhere in sight. Great.

Victor insisted I sit on one of the chaise lounges in the shade, and fussed until he was satisfied that I was comfortable. Within minutes, a very pretty teenager, whom Victor identified as his oldest daughter, came out with a loaded tray, heavy with a pitcher of iced tea and glasses, tiny little sugar-dusted meringue cookies, and a bowl of fat purple grapes. I realized I hadn't eaten or had anything to drink in hours and had a sudden craving for the sweets. I was grateful for the refreshments and for the hiatus in our talk. But now I felt ready to go back on the attack.

"Victor, what do you do with the marijuana? Do you process it here? And what about the money?"

"*Sí,* the money. Follow the money, yes? Nora, you are very *simpática,* and you do good work at the ranch. But you may not write about the marijuana—the now-nonexistent marijuana—or we will sue you and your magazine. And of course fire you. So, since the marijuana does not exist, there is nothing to write about. If—and I say only if—there had been marijuana, there would have been money. But it is nonexistent, so there is none. Here." Victor threw his head back and laughed. His laugh was so light and so free that it was infectious. I smiled in defeat.

I pulled myself somewhat reluctantly out of the chaise. It was beautiful and peaceful here (and I loved those cookies). But I had two huge faxes to read. And undoubtedly the ire of Inspector Nuñez to face.

"Victor," I said slowly as we walked through a heavy oaken door to the front of the house, "I just thought of something. Alan was a stockbroker. Did he move the money around for you? What do they call it, launder it?"

Victor looked at me and put his arm on my shoulder.

"*Por favor,* do not waste your time and cause me and my brother grief by thinking we are to blame for these deaths. And for your accidents. Look closer, Nora, I say again. And be careful. Do not talk about your suspicions. Or your guesses. *Vaya con Dios.*"

I said good-bye and walked toward the garage, where I could see Christian waiting in the Jeep. When I looked back, both Victor and Romero were standing in front of the courtyard door, looking relaxed and without a care in the world. Now what? Follow the money.

Chapter Twenty-One

Wednesday evening

I collapsed onto the bed as soon as I got back to my room. I didn't bother turning down the cotton bedspread or even taking off my sneakers. The adrenaline that had fed my bravado during my meeting with the brothers-from-hell suddenly fled my body, leaving me exhausted and trembling. The aftermath of being chloroformed and the realization that someone had really wanted to hurt me further drained me. And my splinted finger hurt. I didn't exactly fall asleep; it was more like I fell into a coma.

I'm not sure what time it was, but the room was very dark when I awakened to the sound of pounding on my door.

"Coming, I'm coming," I mumbled, as I staggered across the room, then stopped in panic as I remembered the events of the past few days.

"Who's there? What you want?"

I cowered against the wall, too terrified to even look through the spy hole in the door. I could hear shuffling, then murmured voices. I was freezing cold.

"It's me, sweetie," called out a woman's voice. "Allison. And Tom. We've brought you dinner. Open the door. The tray's heavy."

I trembled a bit from relief but still couldn't move.

"Okay, okay. Just a second." I thought I was shouting, but Allison knocked on the door again.

"I know you're there, Nora. It's cold out here. Aren't you hungry?" she asked in a wheedling voice. Hungry. The thought of food made me ill. But I finally moved.

"Sorry. You frightened me."

"Poor lamb." Allison reached over and hugged me, her sheepskin jacket soft and comforting. For a moment I wanted to nestle in.

I stepped back from the door so they could enter, and watched as Tom settled a heavy tray on my coffee table.

"What's all that?" I asked weakly.

"Dinner. We were concerned when you didn't show, figured maybe you'd finally collapsed after your adventures, so Allison convinced that burly chef of yours to let us bring you food."

"Adventures." I smiled at Tom. "I don't really want dinner. I don't feel so good."

"You don't look so good, either, lamb. We'll just leave it with you, to reconsider. I've got a hot bridge date, and now that I know that you're not dying, I'm off. 'Night."

Allison breezed by and was out the door before I even absorbed what she was saying. I watched Tom as he arranged the dishes, then sat beside the table.

"I'm not leaving until you've eaten something, so you might as well . . ."

"Tea." I interrupted. "I just want tea. Wait a minute."

I fumbled around in a cabinet of the tiny kitchenette and managed to find some herbal teabags. Green tea with peach. I set the water to boil while I disappeared into the bathroom.

My God, I looked dreadful. Pale, my eyes narrow slits between swollen lids, my curls sticking up like spikes around my head. I'd seen pictures of Medusa that were more attractive. I did the best I could to tidy up, pulling my T-shirt down so my stomach wouldn't stick out. Going without dinner had some advantages. Something was nagging at me, something Victor said at the end. "Look closer," he'd advised. How much closer?

"Here's your tea," Tom said as I finally emerged, and he pulled out a chair for me. "With lots of sugar."

"Where'd you even find real sugar? I use the phony stuff."

"Tonight you'll use the real thing. You need it."

The tea did taste wonderful, but I gagged a bit looking at the plates of food in front of me.

"Maybe I can get down the soup . . ." I couldn't even remember what was on tonight's menu. Judging from the color, it was tomato something. "But I can't even look at the vegetable curry. I've got to cover it with a plate. Maybe the rice."

"I worry about you. Shit, Nora, I care about you. When you went off so trustingly with that gorilla . . ."

I stood up quickly, too quickly. I felt dizzy.

"Tom, you're great. You're absolutely the kindest, nicest person I've met here. And, um, I am attracted to you. But you should know . . . I'm right in the middle of trying to work out a troubled relationship, one that has meant a lot to me. It may actually be over, but I need to be sure."

"Yeah. I figured from something Allison said."

There was a long silence, and we didn't look at each other. I sat down again and grabbed the hot teacup as if it were a lifeline. It's not as if I'd had scores of men fighting over me. Oh, there've been a handful of serious guys in my life, but no duels have been fought. Nor had I expected any lately, since I felt so fat and unlovely. I sneaked a peek at Tom's face and felt a sweet rush of pleasure at his scowl. Selfish of me. But human. Someone found me attractive.

"Tom . . ." I reached out to touch his arm.

"Hey, it's just ego." He smiled at me. "Or at least, that's part of it. Besides, I'm not sure I buy you and this guy. It sounds to me as if he doesn't really appreciate who you are."

More silence between us. I thought about that. Tom cleared

his throat and replaced the dishes of food on the tray, then set it on the floor, pushing my tote bag aside to make room.

"What the hell's in this bag? Bricks for the oven?"

I hesitated, then decided to just spit it out. After all, Tom and Allison were the only people I really trusted here, weren't they, and I was tired of talking to myself.

"It's all the material I've received about the ranch, and about the people who knew Alan and CeCe best. I've got to finish reading it all tonight." I suddenly gave a huge yawn and scowled at Tom when he laughed. Actually, despite the yawn, I was beginning to wake up.

"I keep coming back to Alan. He's got to be the key here. He was the Cerillos' brother-in-law, a friend of CeCe's—why would someone want him dead?"

"He was irritating as hell, but you don't usually kill someone because they get on your nerves." Tom shrugged his shoulders and looked uncomfortable. "I didn't really know him that well, just as an annual acquaintance, but his main passion was work."

"I heard he had other passions."

"Mostly talk. Oh, he indulged in a little flirting and maybe fooling around, but trust me, wheeling and dealing was what turned him on." Tom got up and walked over to the window, peered out through the dark glass.

"What kind of wheeling and dealing? I know he was a broker, financial adviser, or whatever. Do you think he advised the Cerillos—did I mention they own the ranch, along with another partner? And what's-her-name, you know, Ana, she's the partner's daughter, Dolores's boss."

Tom looked a bit stunned at this outpouring of information, but then shook his head as if to clear it and settled further back in his rocking chair.

I filled Tom in on the afternoon's events.

"So," I continued, "Victor said that Alan was the Cerillo family financial whiz. Do you think he cooked their books?"

"Probably unnecessary. A lot's becoming clearer to me now. This place is a huge cash machine; the owners get paid by guests in U.S. dollars, pay their staff in pesos. They've always farmed, or ranched, land around here, so maybe it's not surprising they bought the ranch. But with what kind of money?"

"We'll get back to that later."

Tom was still working things out in his head. "The Mexican workers—the gardeners, carpenters, massage therapists, beauty types, kitchen staff—they all work cheap. The Cerillos must be raking in the dough."

"Yeah, okay. But if they're into something else here—like selling that grass we saw waving in the fields? That's probably how they got the money to buy the place. Maybe Alan . . ."

"I know someone harvests it. I mean, no one's just going to let it brown out and die." Now he was really talking to himself. "They must have an operation for drying it and processing it. Then they've got to get it across the border. I'm sure they must sell it north of here. What a perfect setup! Shit, they just have to send it into San Diego with someone on staff, or even Alan . . ."

"Maybe. But I see Alan as doing stuff with their money, not transporting pot. You know, he might have established phony accounts for them, investing their money. Laundering, whatever that means."

"Legitimizing illegal profits."

"I'm impressed."

"I read a lot of thrillers."

"How would he do that, Tom? Wait a minute. By setting up phony corporations? Making investments? That sort of thing?"

Tom nodded. "You just can't leave a barrel of unreported cash lying around. Or dump it in your local bank. The Feds get interested in any deposit over ten thousand dollars. They've obviously reinvested a lot of money into the ranch. They're always making improvements. Have you seen the new villas to the west of here? There's rumors that they might sell them as condos, time-shares. Best thing to do with funny money is to put it to work legitimately if you can. Once they get it over the border it could be commingled with honest funds, like in a restaurant, where there's lots of cash floating around. Or in a check-cashing business, or . . ."

"Maybe moved offshore, into a numbered account, and invested in blue-chip stocks. I read mysteries, too. Or even more simply, in a real estate project."

"That could work. Think that's what happened?"

"Do I know? But I do know someone who might know. Once I get my ducks in place." I yawned again. "I've got to finish reading those damned papers tonight. I'd better make the Earl Grey with caffeine this time."

Tom picked up the dinner tray and set it outside the door, to be collected in the morning. He came back into the room and slipped on his jacket, then pulled me to him.

I made no effort to resist his kiss. He tasted deliciously of peach tea, and his lips were soft and sweet. When I found myself responding, I tried to pull back. But Tom's kiss deepened, and as his body hardened against mine, I could feel my heart racing. I needed this, needed to be held, to be desired.

Max was like a ghost, haunting me and popping up when I least expected him. Or wanted him. Tom sensed my withdrawal and touched his lips to my forehead.

"This is going to be continued," he said.

I moved back into his arms, content just to hold and be held. I thought for a moment about asking Tom to stay. I really didn't want to be alone. But that wouldn't be fair to him, would it?

With one last lingering hug, I turned away and picked up my tote bag.

"My homework," I said, smiling as I tossed my research onto

the bed. I cleared my throat and tried to sound normal. "So, who's our candidate for working with Alan? I know he had some sort of business deal, I think real estate, with Buddy, CeCe's husband, but there was someone else involved in that deal. I can't quite remember."

"Simon," said Tom as he left my room. "Not so simple Simon. 'Night Nora."

CHAPTER TWENTY-TWO

Thursday morning

It was two a.m. when I finished reading all the faxes from *MetroScene* and the U.S. Attorney's office. I was so exhausted I could barely reach over to click off the bedside light. But my mind wouldn't click off. I lay there tossing and turning, running over everything again and again.

It was disturbingly quiet. I couldn't even hear the wind, but I sure as hell wasn't going to open a window to the great outdoors. I pulled myself out of bed to check that I'd double-locked the door, then I gave in to my anxiety and dragged a heavy chair against the door.

Back to bed. To tossing and turning. What I wouldn't give for a Valium or an Ambien! I got up again and, with just the dying firelight to guide me, I made some chamomile tea. No help. I tried relaxation techniques that I'd learned in a yoga class. Finally, I just gave up. I shoved an extra pillow behind my head and started reviewing my case.

My case—what grandiosity! But at this point, two days after CeCe's death and three days after Alan's, I really did believe I had a good chance of figuring out who had done what to whom. Inspector Nuñez could check alibis and evidence; I'd concentrate on motives and relationships. Of course, it wouldn't hurt to know about those alibis and evidence. I'd have to hunt up the inspector this morning and try to make a deal with him.

I let the names and faces of the people who knew Alan and

CeCe, my acquaintances, a few now my friends, float in and around my brain. It was like looking through a kaleidoscope. If I held still, their faces formed perfect side-by-side pictures. If I turned my head on the pillow, they began to overlap, and re-arrange themselves, and form new patterns. Was Simon really jealous of Alan? Was he in a real estate deal with him? Did CeCe know or suspect who killed Alan? What about Allison? Had she had an affair with Alan? With Simon? And Tom . . . Phoebe . . . where did they fit into the picture? I rather believed Victor Cerillo. He was creepy, and made me nervous (and could make me unemployed), and may have had a booming career as a marijuana merchant, but I didn't think he killed Alan or CeCe.

My head ached. I had kept my eyes closed while watching my interior kaleidoscope, and I guess I finally drifted off. Not that I benefited greatly from my sleep. I dozed fitfully off and on through what remained of the night. My dreams were horrific. In one, someone was smothering me with a pillow. I was flailing around helplessly while faceless, thin, leotard-clad women were oblivious, dancing around me in an aerobic routine.

Glad as I was that morning had finally come, I was nevertheless unprepared for the pounding on my door while I was in the bathroom. It was barely seven a.m.

"What is it? Who is it?" I shouted, groggy and irritable.

A voice shouted back that it was Inspector Enrique Nuñez and I should open the door at once. I got some small satisfaction out of making him wait in the cold while I checked through the window to be sure it was indeed he, pulled on some sweats over the T-shirt I'd slept in, and finally maneuvered the chair away from the door.

"I am sorry to disturb you so early, *Señorita*," he said with obvious pleasure, "but you were very difficult to find yesterday." He glanced curiously around the messy room, then seated himself comfortably at the table.

I did feel a bit guilty about having avoided him all of yesterday. "Do you want some tea before we talk?"

He shook his head no and sat quietly, waiting for me to boil the water. The minute I sat down with my Lemon Zinger tea, he laid into me. Beneath his oh-so-polite manner I could feel the air crackle: he was understandably furious that I hadn't reported either of my attacks, indeed, had left while he was on the way to interview me after my herbal wrap. I hadn't told him I was "investigating" his case. I hadn't told him anything. I just kept nodding my agreement. He was right: I hadn't told him anything. And although I was uneasy and even felt guilty about deceiving him, I didn't want to tell him now either.

As I emerged out of my early morning fog, I realized that the papers scattered all over the bed and floor were the faxes from *MetroScene* and the U.S. Attorney's office. I casually moved over to the bed as if to tidy the room, but the good inspector was too sharp and quick. He began to scoop up the papers and scan them. I grabbed them back from him and stuffed them into my tote bag. My heart beat furiously as I wondered whether to challenge him. Memories of the movie *Traffic* with its scenes set in a Mexican jail ran through my mind. I didn't want to go there.

"That's my private property, Inspector," I said anxiously. "Do you have a warrant, or whatever it's called in Mexico? I didn't give you permission . . ."

"Is there information in that material that would be damaging to one of your friends? I believe you are aware of such a thing called 'obstruction of justice,' *Señorita* Nora. I could make things very difficult for you here. Or you could assist the police." His voice was very gentle.

" 'Assist the police.' Is that like saying you're going to arrest me?" *Be nice, Nora.* "Maybe I shouldn't speak further to you without my lawyer." *How easily can I get in touch with Max?* I wondered. Would he refer me to a local lawyer? Dammit, I needed him now!

Nuñez sighed deeply and plucked at his mustache, then sat down again. We stared at each other. Impasse. I broke first.

"I have a meeting with the chef at eight forty-five. Is that okay?"

"*Señorita* Nora, if I may. I am a careful investigator. I have found whatever evidence there has been to find, I have checked alibis and I have talked with all of the staff and the guests. I was assigned to this case because my English is so much better than other officers. Unfortunately, however, sorting out the relationships in this drama are beyond my talents. If I had a month, perhaps . . . But unless I can give good reasons to my *comandante*, and . . ." He sighed again, even more deeply, "to the American authorities, almost everyone will leave here in two days. At the end of their never-to-be-forgotten week at a spa. Every expensive lawyer in California, Texas, even New York has been calling my office, demanding information and the promise that their client can go home. I need a shortcut, and you may be it. So, can we speak honestly?"

My dream come true. If I could believe it.

"My part of it seems clear," I said hesitantly. "I tell you everything I know and think. And your part?"

Nuñez gave a bark of a laugh.

"Firstly, I will promise not to arrest you." He continued to chuckle to himself. I did not smile. "Next, *Señorita* Nora, I will share enough information with you so that you can write your article by tomorrow. Yes, I know about that magazine and your assignment. This is not a game, *Señorita*, in which you decide what information you share with me. Two people have died."

"How dare you suggest I'm playing a game! I know all too well that two people have died. I watched one of them die. Someone I was genuinely fond of. And Alan Nardy—I didn't know him, and don't much like what I now know of him—but no one should die like that, abandoned and alone. They were murdered with gratuitous cruelty, probably by someone I know, and maybe even like."

"Why not forget this 'investigation,' *Señorita* Nora? You've been threatened, and I'm sure that while you are very courageous, you must be just a little bit frightened. Let it go. Let me do my work, without tripping over you."

"It's true I'm a little bit frightened. Actually, I'm scared out of my wits. But I'm going to write my article, which does involve poking my nose into places it may not belong. It's important to me professionally. And personally: I was raised to want the truth."

I got up and started to make more tea.

"It's strange, you know," I said more calmly. "Maybe I seem courageous because I've never really thought my life was in danger, despite the 'accidents' I've been having. I could have been badly hurt. Both times. But I feel as if I've just been warned off. Without a sense of—malevolence. Directed at me."

"Do not count on this 'feeling' of yours. It may not be trustworthy."

"Inspector Nuñez," I said formally. "I will share the information my sources have gathered for me . . . in return for your information. I can see that it makes sense, for both of us. Mostly for you." He had the courtesy to look a little uncomfortable. "I'll make a copy of this material at the office and give it to you. I have ranch business to attend to all morning, but perhaps we could meet around two this afternoon? Here?"

"Do you plan on interviewing anyone else before we meet?" asked the inspector, smiling slightly.

I smiled back and shook my head emphatically. Not unless I got the chance to.

After he left, I pillaged my refrigerator and cupboard for

whatever I could find to eat. It wasn't exactly a food writer's dream: a cup of cold sorrel soup left over from dinner a few nights ago, a piece of stale multigrain bread, some very good local goat cheese, and two promising peaches. I saved a frozen brownie for my afternoon jitters.

I sat down with my notes for the staff meeting and my late morning lecture to the guests. The meeting with Miguel would be easy. We'd go over the menus for the rest of the week, talk about what hasn't been successful so far, then work on next week's menus. With the days getting colder, I should probably add a few hot soups.

Planning for my lectures was more complicated. Usually, by this time in the week, we'd have had three or four classes, some demonstrations of cooking techniques, and some tryouts of low calorie vegetarian dishes. But given the circumstances, with one guest falling off a mountain and another poisoned by a health drink, we'd canceled the last few days' sessions. And I couldn't be sure anyone would actually show up to taste my food today. They might be a bit leery of my offerings. I'd better prepare for my usual group of ten or twelve, and hope for six.

Once I got into it, I spent a very happy hour nibbling at breakfast and working on some of the recipes I intended to use in the ranch cookbook as well as on the menu. It always relaxed me to plan and plot about food. I thought I'd add a simple, hearty Mexican zucchini soup that would give me the opportunity to show the class how to handle jalapeños and other chilies without burning their hands or lips (cold water's the key!). Since I've been feeling anxious, maybe I'd make one of my favorite "comfort" dishes: baked acorn squash stuffed with sautéed chopped apples, onions, and nuts mixed with cottage cheese, grated cheese, lemon juice, and currants. Lots of yummy carbs. I'd sprinkle the top with cinnamon and hope there'd be enough time to bake them.

Feeling much happier now that I'd actually earned some of my consulting fee, I raced out for my meetings, just remembering in time to grab my little digital camera. Maybe I'd have a moment to take some pictures for the *MetroScene* article. Due tomorrow, Nora. Remember?

CHAPTER TWENTY-THREE

Thursday, midday

The morning went fast. Miguel spent only five minutes or so flexing his macho muscles, and we agreed fairly amicably about what dishes to drop and add. The class was successful, too. It was surprisingly well attended: twenty-four women and a handful of men. Perhaps everyone wanted to stay together in a group. As I suspected it would be, the stuffed squash (I'd have to think of a punchy name for it) was a hit. All of the demonstration ones were demolished, and a cold two-melon soup I'd thrown together at the last minute was gobbled up as dessert.

Since it had turned into a brilliantly sunny, if chilly, day, I took my lunch tray to one of the tables outside the dining room and pulled out the background faxes from Max's office. They were camouflage, really, to discourage anyone from joining me. I needed some quiet time to think. I'd reviewed them all quite thoroughly last night, and while they told me more than I really wanted to know about Phoebe's love life (as flamboyant as she looked: the gossip columns were full of her exploits), Jody and Simon's finances (he was a gambler in the commodities market, but she was still in charge of their bankbooks, and I couldn't even imagine how Max's staff got that information), and Allison's career ethics (some questions had been raised, to my disappointment), I had found no smoking gun. Nor could I find out anything about Tom or CeCe, other than what was on the surface.

I'd hoped to have found a definite business connection between Alan and one of the "posse." As much as I enjoyed their company (well, no, not Simon's), it seemed all too logical that one of them was responsible for Alan and CeCe's deaths. But the potential villains were few. I refused to think Tom or Allison could have been involved. They were my friends. Actually, Tom and Phoebe seemed completely clear of extracurricular dealings with Alan. Allison didn't appear to have any business relationship to him either, although they'd had a brief affair a few years earlier. Jody and Alan had, of course, been lovers, but that was before Simon, and she clearly adored Simon. Who, according to Tom, had been in some sort of real estate deal with Alan. As had CeCe's husband, Buddy. Interestingly, that hadn't shown up in the background checks.

It seemed so convoluted. Too convoluted. What was it that Dennis always said at magazine staff meetings? KISS—keep it simple, stupid. Why did I feel I was making this more complicated than it was?

My head spinning, I decided to let my information overload settle for a while. I ran off a copy of the faxes up at the office and started back to my room to meet with Nuñez.

"Nora, wait up," called Tom, loping toward me from the dining room. He looked like an overgrown college boy with his beat-up sweatpants and worn T-shirt, tousled hair, and confident grin.

"Tom," I said, "what did you mean last night?"

"About continuing where we left off?" he asked, grinning even more broadly.

I smiled up at him.

"No, Tom, about Simon having been in a deal with Alan."

"Ah, that. Well, Alan was getting tired of being a small town financial guy. His biggest clients, after all, were his brothers-in-law. He had met CeCe's husband once, when Buddy joined them for dinner in San Diego, and they got to talking about a new town Buddy was planning with a consortium, somewhere between Dallas and Fort Worth. Alan liked the sound of it. He thought he'd be a player. Big time. That was last year. Actually, I know all about this because he asked me if I wanted in, but I don't have that kind of money. I can't believe Alan did either. I'm pretty sure Buddy asked Simon, too. But I don't know where it stands now."

More complications. I waved good-bye to Tom and told him I'd see him at dinner. I liked Tom and was certainly attracted to him. But did I trust him? Feeling as fat and awkward as I did, it was sometimes hard to believe that a good-looking, interesting, available male would find me desirable. Then, there was Max . . .

When I reached my casita, Nuñez was sitting on the small stone terrace. I handed the inspector the copies I'd made and dropped my tote bag on the outdoor table. It was warm in the sun now, so I brought out the pitcher of orange-spice iced tea I'd had chilling, and Nuñez and I sat quietly sipping our tea while he read my papers and I looked at his.

"This reads like a summary," I complained.

Nuñez smiled his little smile.

"It took me a long time to translate my notes for you, *Señorita* Nora. I think you will find all you need there."

He seemed to think something was a huge joke. Was he toying with me? Despite his supposed candor and warmth, could he think I was involved in murder?

In the meantime, he was reading *MetroScene's* research into the history of the ranch and its ownership by the Cerillos and Carlos Tamayo.

"Did you know any of that?" I asked the inspector.

He smiled at me broadly. "Half of my family works here. The ranch is the biggest employer, next to the Tecate beer factory, in this part of Baja. Of course I knew." He skipped over to the background material on the "cast of characters," courtesy of the U.S. Attorney's office. I had a quick, unhappy feeling that I might have gotten Max in trouble. I knew that his sending me this material was not exactly kosher.

I skimmed through the alibis. Great, no one had one. At least, no one had a confirmed one.

"You knew all of this!" I cried, skipping through the inspector's notes. "About Alan's activities, and that slimy Joe, and all. And why that little amused smirk?"

"I am not laughing at you, *Señorita* Nora. But yes, I know now as a fact that Alan Nardy took money over the border for Mariana's brothers. We've suspected that for a long time. Our tax bureau has been engaged in their own quiet investigation for months. But we've never been able to prove it wasn't legitimate money from Rancho profits. Although there was some of that, too. And that 'slimy Joe,' as you call the instructor here, has his own small side business, reasonably profitable, providing marijuana and more glamorous drugs to select guests as well as to his contacts in town. We are checking into his sources, although . . . But none of this, I do not think, is connected to the deaths of Alan Nardy or your friend Cecilia.

"My information, by the way, was of great value to the office of the U.S. Attorney. We were put in touch with them by the Southern District office in New York City; there is some concern about the mixture of drugs and fitness spas. They think it unhealthy." He started to laugh at this point, and I broke down and joined him. It did seem ridiculous.

Of course I knew the answer, but I had to ask the question.

"Why was the U.S. Attorney's office in New York involved? And knew to get in touch with you?"

Inspector Nuñez looked at me in a benign, almost avuncular fashion.

"I know that according to your movies and detective stories,

Mexican police are corrupt at worst, stupid at best." He waved away my attempt to deny these all-too-true beliefs. "Did you really think that after a major crime, the death of a man we have long suspected of helping to cheat our country of legitimate taxes hiding profits from illegal activities, we would not examine every document sent to or from here? And too," he added, "a U.S. Attorney, the chief of the Major Crime Unit in faraway New York City, has been concerned about the safety of an amateur investigator."

"Dammit, won't he ever believe I can take care of myself?"

Nuñez's eyes dropped to the splint on my finger but said nothing. I wondered how much brilliant detective work he was responsible for, and how much he'd been guided by Max.

"I should think, *Señorita,* that you should be gratified by his concern. But then, you can discuss it with him when you next speak."

He gathered his share of the papers together, shook my hand, and practically ran off the terrace toward the spa office beyond. I sat still. *When we next speak.*

Right now, Max was the last person I wanted to speak to. It was hard for me to lie to him, and he seemed to sense it with as much acuity as if he were watching my nose grow. And I didn't want to tell him about the threats to me. This was my challenge, my job to do. So I'd better get on with it.

CHAPTER TWENTY-FOUR

Thursday afternoon

I might not have wanted to speak to Max, but I needed to speak to someone. It couldn't be my mother; at the very least, I'd hear, "What are you doing? Are you crazy? Do you want to get yourself killed?" I needed warmth and support, if not necessarily approval.

I wandered over to where the "Backs and Bellies" class would soon begin, but there was no one I knew around. Actually, there were no women milling around outside the gym. All were huddled together inside—safety in numbers, I guess. I looked in the lodge and dining room area for Allison, but she was nowhere to be found. Anyway, I was feeling lonely for an old friend, one who knew my history and quirks and to whom I didn't have to explain myself.

I wanted some privacy for my phone call and didn't feel like trekking into town, so I walked up the hill to the villas, huffing and puffing maybe a little less than in the past, to my favorite pool area. I made sure I remained in sight of the gardeners and workmen in the area, but nevertheless started at every random sound. Rabbits running across the road sent my heart racing. In safer times, only last week, I'd liked to swim up here, out of sight of the ultrathin guests. A bonus was that I'd discovered a phone, one of the few remote phones at the spa, near a distant chaise in the shade. I suppose it was for the use of those workaholics who needed to stay in touch with their offices as they sunbathed. I'm a bit of a workaholic myself, and it drove me crazy that my cell phone wouldn't work here. Instead of relaxing me, it made me crazier. I placed a collect call to Judith.

Aside from being my agent, Judith was my best friend and confidante. This was despite the fact that she's never really understood what continues to bond me to Max. She likes him a lot but strongly believes I'd be better off without him. She thinks he's too critical of me and doesn't really "get" me. She's wrong. I think. But no matter what limb I've ever crawled out on, Judith's always been there to coax me back to safety. I was counting on her loyalty and calm good sense.

"What the hell's going on, Nora?" she screeched. "I keep getting these hysterical bulletins from your mother about murder and poisoning. She says I forced you to take this job, and it's my fault if you get killed. And Max says . . ."

"Whoa, Judith. I've called you for loving support, not to be yelled at. And this conversation is just between us, okay? Nothing goes back to Rose, much less to Max. I can predict what they'll say, but I need you right now."

"At least I know you're alive," she grumbled. I let that pass. "Let's take it from the top, Nora," she said more calmly. "I read about that guy dying on top of the mountain, and about the woman being poisoned. Dennis called to say he'd asked you to write a piece about it all for *MetroScene*. I cut you a good deal, incidentally." I made noises of approval. "So now what? You doing more than just an 'I was there' story?"

"Well, actually . . ."

"Nora. Don't mess around with this. Shit, I've been waiting since college for your mother's 'the truth-will-set-us-free' genes to pop out in you. It's happened, hasn't it? You're going to meddle and put yourself in danger and . . ."

"Hold on. Just listen up before you scold me."

It was such a relief to unload, to talk about the people I'd met, my theories, my concerns . . . even my attraction to Tom, which predictably made Judith very happy. I told her about everything except the threats to my life. Small omission.

"Nora, have you drifted off somewhere?"

"See, Judith, I started off thinking that I'd focus the article on Alan, and on his carrying drug money over the border for his brothers-in-law, then laundering that money somehow. I even met the Cerillo brothers."

I told Judith about my afternoon visit to Alan Nardy's in-laws and the veiled threats I'd received. "One brother was mute, the other was inordinately charming. I don't know which scared me more. At any rate, I have a few ideas as to how the money may have been laundered, and Inspector Nuñez has pretty much acknowledged Alan's activities. Although," I added slowly, "I suppose I'll have to keep saying 'alleged' in the article."

"I'm changing my mind about your doing this article. It's too dangerous."

"It won't be dangerous. I'll just do an 'I was there' piece." (Liar! My nose must be growing.) "I'll start writing it tonight, after another few interviews. Thanks to research I got from the magazine, and background stuff from Max's office, I've learned that Simon and CeCe's husband, Buddy, had some sort of real estate connection, and possibly Alan was involved too. I wish I understood more about money laundering and investments."

"Write the damned article, Nora. It's due tomorrow night. Play detective next week."

"They'll all be gone next week." I felt a pang of regret. I'd miss Allison and Tom. And what if the crimes weren't solved by then? Should I leave too?

"I just thought of something," I said. "Do you know a Phoebe Hollis? She's in PR, a tall, very dramatic-looking high-energy type."

"I've heard of her. Does mostly fashion stuff. She's supposed to be ruthless about getting what she wants." I could hear an edginess in Judith's voice. "Look, I've got a lunch date with clients at Le Bernardin, and the car service has been waiting downstairs for ages, so just promise me . . ."

"The article will be done on time, I promise." I knew that that wasn't what Judith wanted me to promise. "Love you, Jude." I hung up before I could be admonished or warned again. Simon first. Then Phoebe.

CHAPTER TWENTY-FIVE

Later Thursday afternoon

I knew Simon and Jody were staying in a villa and felt sure that it would be one of the newest ones, on the westerly side of the hill. I wandered around for the next twenty minutes, surprising one guest sunbathing in the buff on his patio and interrupting a tête-à-tête—or new yoga workout—between two others, then struck gold.

The villa the Neels had rented was magnificent: built of stone and stucco, it had a curved stone patio cantilevered over the valley, with Mount Cuchuma as a sun-streaked backdrop. I knew it was their villa because of Simon's gray cashmere sweater draped over a chair and Jody's familiar red tote bag on the patio table. But they were nowhere in sight. I hesitated, reluctant to interrupt an afternoon nap or more intimate scene within, yet unwilling to retreat without speaking to Simon. The sun was really hot on the exposed patio, and I tried to take shelter behind a spindly locust tree.

"I'm not blaming you, Si, I told you that a million times. Don't be so angry." Jody's voice, on the edge of hysteria, came closer to where I was standing. They must be in the front kitchen area. I ducked farther down behind the retaining wall of the patio, slipping a bit on the gravel path. The tiny yellow flowers of the chamomile plant covered the slope, which was dotted with spiky aromatic shrubs. I grabbed onto one to keep from sliding further. Its rough-edged leaves dug into my palm, and I winced. Jody and Simon were yelling at each other too loudly to have heard me slip.

"Bullshit! You are blaming me! You and your mother both. It wasn't my fault the deal fell apart. Buddy swore it was a sure thing, that the governor had given his word that the new town would be approved on our land. You okayed the investment . . ."

"I knew how much you wanted to do it, Simon."

"Oh, you're so good to me, Jody. Such a loving, supportive wife. It makes me want to puke. Nardy told me not to go to you for the money, that you'd hold it over my head if anything went wrong. He knew you, all right. He knew something about everyone, didn't he? Irritating son of a bitch. Stop crying, for God's sake. And stop backing away like I'm going to hurt you."

"Please don't be mad, Simon. I just wanted to protect you from Alan. I knew he was jealous of you. I didn't trust him about pulling you into that deal. And he was terrible about money. I did tell you that, didn't I? Untrustworthy, careless . . ."

"That's a joke, right? He was a stockbroker, dammit. I didn't believe you. I still don't. I thought you were covering up that you were still in love with him."

"Simon, you couldn't have thought . . . why didn't you tell me? You must know how much I love you. I was fond of Alan. He was my first boyfriend, but I love you."

Jody's wailing stopped short. I hoped Simon was kissing her, not throttling her. A good opportunity to quickly get away.

I scrambled down the hill, stumbling over the uneven ground. I made my way as quickly as I could back to the phone near the pool, and was relieved to see that there was only one sunbather there, who looked as if she was in a coma. I called *MetroScene* and spoke to Danny, just to be sure the arrangements were still set. Unlike my darling Judith, Danny egged me on, telling me what I wanted to hear: that there was no danger involved in my writing an investigative piece and that my future at the magazine could be positively affected. He got me to promise to send the piece tomorrow night, and to e-mail pictures as well.

Finally, I dug out Mariana Cerillo's phone number from my bag, hoping she'd remember our planned telephone interview. At first I thought she wasn't in, but after the sixth ring, just as the answering machine cut in, a light voice said *"Bueno."*

I explained again who I was and that we'd spoken right after her husband's tragic death, then went on to say in very careful English that I was writing an article that with any luck would expose the truth about how Alan had died. (I didn't mention that I would also expose how he made the money to support her in La Jolla, and his relationship with her brothers.) Mariana, however, was not an innocent. And her English was perfect.

"I know exactly who you are, *Señorita* Franke, and my brother Victor told me not to speak to you. But I will now decide if I will."

"Mariana, if I may, *Señora* Nardy, I am not interested in learning anything about Alan's relationship with your brothers. I just want to know about a business deal that your husband appears to have had with Buddy Clayton and Simon Neel. Mr. Clayton's wife, CeCe, and Mr. Neel are also guests here. Have you met them? Did they arrange to be here at this time to talk about their plans?"

A decidedly unladylike snort was Mariana's response.

"Plans? What plans? Nothing is left of those stupid plans. Or of the money. That Texas idiot Buddy convinced my Alan to invest with him, even though I begged Alan not to listen to him. Alan had dreams of becoming a big deal. And that other one, Neel, he was the worst. He called Alan night and day, kept threatening to tell the authorities that Alan was doing illegal things if Alan didn't get the money back from Buddy. How could he do that? My poor Alan was out of his depth. I tried to have him call my brothers for help, but he was too proud. I tell you this because I am happy to put Simon and Buddy in trouble. And because I want you to understand about Alan . . ."

Wow. This lady's voice was venomous and cold with rage. I did love the way she said "Alan," though. Sort of "Alyan."

"Surely your brothers won't permit you and your son to lose your home, or be at risk . . ."

"Of course not. We will probably move back to La Paz, to a house on one of Victor's properties. My family will take care of us." Her voice hardened. "They are now convinced that they were right, that I should never have married Alan, that a woman cannot be trusted to make her own decisions about such a thing as marriage. I suppose I will have to listen to Victor from now on. Another tragedy."

"Did you get the idea that Buddy or Simon had stolen the money, *Señora?* Or was it just a bad business deal that fell through?"

"I do not think anyone stole the money, Ms. Franke. But that Simon, he did not believe Alan. He was very rude, not at all *simpático*. Not even when he speaks to me. I have told you all that I can, *Señorita*. I will not tell my brothers I speak to you. They do not trust you, although Victor does like you. But I think you will be fired soon. *Adiós.*"

CHAPTER TWENTY-SIX

Late Thursday afternoon

I sat beside the pool for a long while, thinking about my conversations with Judith, Danny, and Mariana, and what I'd overheard between Jody and Simon. I wondered if I should forget about talking to Phoebe and just go with what I had. I felt edgy and restless, unable to concentrate. Was I doing any good here? Would it help to write the article I was planning? As soon as I finished my story I'd consider leaving, I thought.

I'd probably feel better once I started to get my thoughts on paper, I decided. There was no point to worrying if Mariana was right, that I was about to be fired. But I'd hate to go home with my tail between my legs. Whoa . . . what home? I'd sublet my apartment to Leslie for three months. Could I bear moving back in with Rose? At the very least, sending in the *MetroScene* article would ensure I had a job in New York.

The sun had moved across the patio, leaving me partially in the shade, and I began to feel the late afternoon chill. Thinking to save myself a long walk, I called the front desk and asked if I had received any more faxes or phone calls. The answer was no, but Inspector Nuñez was looking for me. More good news.

I pulled myself up from the comfortable chaise and slowly made my way down the hill to find Nuñez. And now, now that I was no longer looking for her, I immediately saw Phoebe. She was dressed in tennis whites, her voluminous hair pulled back in a tidy thick braid. She looked tired but as crisp and immaculate as ever.

"Wait up, Phoebe," I called impulsively. "Got a minute?"

She hesitated, then shrugged.

"I need to drink something," she called back. "Might as well go to my hacienda."

I nodded and followed as she turned toward a cluster of pretty wood-and-stone cottages beside the creek. By the time I reached her tiny patio, she had thrown her racket and towel down on a chair and disappeared inside. I wandered around the patio, restless.

"I must be next on your list." Phoebe had brought a pitcher of iced tea and two glasses out with her, and downed half of her glass while still standing. She looked at me with amusement. "I made this myself, Nora. It's perfectly safe. Drink up."

I toasted her and sipped the cold tea.

"I'm not sure why you're here," she said, sitting on the bench surrounding the patio. "I don't know what I can tell you that I didn't tell the inspector. Or why I should tell you anything," she added with her customary acerbity.

"I thought you could give me some more personal insight as to why Alan and CeCe were killed. What connected them?"

She smiled . . . more of a smirk, actually. "Surely Allison has told you all about them. No? Well, there wasn't really that much to tell. CeCe was very fond of Alan. She called him a cuddly teddy bear. And so he was, with claws." She held the cold glass to her temples. "Of course, CeCe's experiences with men were limited. She was used to being adored and pampered. She didn't see Alan as the manipulative, selfish bastard that he was."

I laughed. "Don't hold back, Phoebe. Let me know what you really thought of him."

She smiled, an open, genuine smile for the first time since I'd met her.

"I never could get it, Nora. Why CeCe, Jody, Allison, and half a dozen other women here fawned over him. He really did like women, though. Talked to women. Listened to women. Maybe that was it."

She paused while pouring more tea into our glasses, then finally said, "The only connection I know of between Alan and CeCe, aside from being friends here, was CeCe's husband, Buddy. He and Alan had some sort of real estate deal going; Simon was part of it too. They asked Tom to go in on it with them. Don't think he did. Allison and I were, of course, the little women, and weren't invited."

"Would you have been interested?" I asked. "It sounds as if you didn't trust Alan."

"I didn't. And no, I didn't—don't—have that kind of money to invest. But . . ." she smiled at me again. ". . . I hate being left out of things."

"Well, I've heard about that deal between the 'boys,' " I acknowledged. "Nothing new there, I'm afraid." Now was my turn to hesitate. I'd never make a good investigative reporter; I hated to get people mad at me.

"Phoebe, are you aware of Joey's extracurricular stuff? His dealing, maybe even money laundering?"

Phoebe's jaw tightened, and her gorgeous tinted green contact lenses glared at me. She stood and, without a word, walked back into the hacienda.

Once again I got up reluctantly from a comfortable seat in the shade. I had thought Phoebe had been unusually pleasant and cooperative; I guess I hit the wrong—or right—note. And did I really care? Joey might be a creep and might deal in pot or fancier designer drugs, but I honestly didn't think he had anything to do with Alan's—or CeCe's—death.

It would, however, add some vivid color to my story. I must call the magazine's lawyers and find out how much I could say, or insinuate, without getting into a lawsuit. Time to wake my laptop up from its nap.

I crossed the bridge over the creek, heading for my casita. Inspector Nuñez was ahead of me, walking past my casita. I called out his name and waved, but he disappeared beyond a clump of trees.

As I unlocked the door to the casita, I noticed an envelope on the floor that had clearly been shoved under the door. The cursive script on the sheet of paper inside was full of flourishes and not too easy to read. But I finally managed to decipher the handwriting:

My dear Señorita Nora: Despite your suspicions of me, I did appreciate truly your giving to me the background material. And so I am happy to share with you the results of the medical examiner's office. It will, at any rate, soon be public information since the San Diego newspapers have somehow been told.

Alan Nardy died from a cerebral hemorrhage from hitting his head on a rock when he fell, and from exposure too. No surprise, no? Your friend Cecilia drank the almond milk spiced with just a few drops of nicotine sulfate. She must have been very sensitive, poor soul, for the poison rarely kills people that rapidly. Bugs on roses, however, it kills very quickly. Everything stops when you drink this: all the muscles, nerves, everything. So now we know. Except we do not yet know who or what caused Alan Nardy to fall from the mountain peak, or who dropped the poison into Cecilia's cup. But we will find out, yes?

Your friend, Enrique Nuñez.

I felt sick, devastated. It had been bad enough watching CeCe become paralyzed, then die after convulsions had shaken her tiny body. Bad enough saying the words, hearing about Buddy's arrival here, about his waiting to take her body home. And certainly a nightmare to think of those twin baby boys she so adored, now without their mother. But hearing it confirmed that someone, someone here, someone I'm sure I knew, deliberately released little droplets of death in her drink. That filled me with rage.

I crumbled the letter in my fist. I was going to get the son of a bitch. I was going to lay on such heavy stuff in my article, so many details and so much dirt, that it would be totally clear who the bastard was. I hoped. Right now, I wasn't certain. But I did have my suspicions. Let the lawyers worry about getting sued.

My growling stomach reminded me that it was dinnertime. I'd lost another half a day. So many things I'd meant to do. Well, at least Judith would keep Rose and Max off my back for a while. For all I knew, Max and Nuñez were in constant touch.

I took a quick shower and changed into jeans and a black cashmere tunic. Cheered at least by how much better my clothes were fitting, I walked quickly to the lodge. No need to be wary of walking alone. The paths were filled with guests. It seemed people had come out of hiding, reaching for community.

It was "cocktail" time in the lodge, the first time I'd been back there since CeCe's death. Allison and what remained of her group would be there, along with most of the other guests. Who had access to nicotine poison? Or who smoked and could distill the nicotine? I assumed one could do that; another query for my checker at the magazine. I wished I could get onto the Internet on my laptop. Wireless technology had not yet reached the cottages.

I spotted Allison as soon as I entered the lodge. Her long, silvery blonde hair was like a magnet, and her extra inches made her immediately visible among the other women in the room. She caught sight of me and waved me over.

"Been looking for you all day, Nora," she called.

I waved back and made my way through the dozens of other hungry guests to get to Allison and the hors d'oeuvre table. I grabbed a handful of cut-up strips of carrots and jicama and stopped to chat briefly with a few women who'd been in some of my classes, then met Tom's eyes across the table. He smiled and held out a glass to me.

"Iced tea," he said. "From my hands to yours."

He pointed at the large sign on the table: ALL FOOD AND BEVERAGES ARE FRESHLY MADE AND SUPERVISED.

I was still too disturbed by the thought of liquid nicotine to joke back, but I did make an attempt at a smile. Tom walked around the table to join me.

"Allison and I wanted to ask you to join us all tomorrow night," he said. "We've made kind of a ritual of Friday night dinners out—we go to Christina's, up the road. To celebrate our last night here. Margaritas and other forbidden fruit." He paused, frowning. "There'll be fewer of us this year. I guess we'll have some friends to toast and say good-bye to."

"She may be scared to be seen with us, Tommy lamb. Maybe Nora thinks we're being knocked off one at a time." Allison had come up behind us as we were speaking.

"I'm fearless," I replied grimly. "They haven't managed to kill me yet." No one said anything. "What if you have to leave here not knowing who was responsible?" I asked. "Never knowing? Could you ever return?"

Neither Tom nor Allison answered.

"Let's go to dinner," Allison finally said, hooking her arms through ours. We marched off, a seemingly united front.

CHAPTER TWENTY-SEVEN

Thursday dinner

Dinner was not a lot of laughs. Phoebe was sitting at the staff table with Joey when we came in, so we took a small table and figured Jody and Simon would fend for themselves. Joey and Phoebe had both glared at me when I walked by their table, and I glared back. I was not the sleazy one in this group. Tomorrow night's margarita dinner might be the last this group shared. It seemed so sad and curiously anticlimactic.

"Not the week I'd hoped we'd enjoy together, lamb," said Allison. "But," she added with more energy, "there's still tomorrow night and Saturday morning."

"What happens Saturday morning?" I asked.

"I swear I'm going to get you up that mountain before I go. You'll love it once you do it . . . I promise. There's a meditation hike I usually take on Saturdays, at dawn, but I'll make the ultimate sacrifice and climb up with you a bit later; we'll take it real slow. Tom, will you join us?"

"If you promise not to hug a tree when you come down," he said.

"No tree hugging, although I always do part of the yoga 'salute to the sun' when I reach the top."

"I'd like to learn that," I said with more enthusiasm than I'd had all evening. "I've just started taking some yoga classes with Rachel, and she was talking about the different classic poses. I'll go for it."

I was surprised at myself; Mount Cuchuma had loomed large these last few weeks, first because of its size, and then because of Alan's death. But I really did want to make the climb, and the thought of going up with Allison and Tom's encouragement, along with yoga stretches at the top, pleased me.

"Dinner tomorrow night sounds lovely," I said, "but I'll be able to do it only if I finish my article. Truth is, I haven't even started it yet. I've got tonight, after dinner, and most of tomorrow. I only have one class left and a meeting at lunchtime."

"So, what's your pitch going to be on all of this, Nora? What have you dug up?" asked Tom. "Will you hint at who you think committed the crimes?"

I didn't feel constrained to keep the inspector's information secret, not if it would be all over the San Diego papers in the morning.

"Alan died of a cerebral hemorrhage," I said quietly. "He probably never regained consciousness after getting knocked out in the fall, and the overnight cold finished him off." Something occurred to me for the first time. "You know, his death might not have been deliberate, at least not at first. Leaving him there unconscious, though, that's something else. But CeCe . . ." I got mad all over again, furious at the ugliness of her death, at the cruel deliberateness of her killer.

"What about CeCe?" Allison's voice was harsh, rough at the edges.

"Nicotine poison."

"You mean from cigarettes?" Allison looked bewildered. "But she didn't smoke."

I just shook my head.

Tom asked gently, "Liquid nicotine poison? In her drink?"

I nodded and cleared my throat. "It's evidently used to kill bugs on plants, rose plants mostly. And there are lots of roses around here. I assume Inspector Nuñez is checking the greenhouses on the grounds and the local nurseries."

"Why? That's still the question. Why CeCe?" Allison sat staring into space, her eyes glazed over.

"Why are you asking about CeCe? Why not wonder about Alan?" I asked.

Allison snapped back into focus.

"Because Alan was capable of irritating the hell out of any number of people. For any number of reasons. Everyone loved CeCe."

"Obviously not everyone," said Tom.

We'd all stopped eating by now, the special Thursday night treat of steamed local fish with tomatoes and herbs, and its accompaniments of steamed vegetables and savory brown rice, sat practically untouched on our plates. I motioned to our waitress to wrap up my dinner. The others weren't interested, but I'd need food later if I planned to work tonight. Neither Tom nor Allison seemed inclined to linger, and we left the table as soon as I got my wrapped dinner.

On our way out of the dining room, Tom stopped to speak to Jody and Simon, reminding them about dinner plans at Christina's tomorrow night. I stood beside him, smiling blandly at Jody. Something kept tickling at the edge of my mind. I had had that same sense of discomfort—like a fragment of a lost memory—when I'd stopped by their villa earlier in the day. Was it something they had said, that I'd overheard? Something I'd seen? As quickly as it had entered my mind, it vanished. What Rose calls a "senior moment," but I guess thirty-somethings were susceptible too.

I said good night to Allison, who had joined another table for dessert, and gave only token resistance to Tom when he insisted on walking me home. He knew my work agenda and didn't suggest coming in. I was so grateful for his understanding and his support that I gave him an enthusiastic one-armed hug (the other arm was clutching my dinner and my ubiquitous hot pink tote bag). As I put the bag down on my coffee table, the elusive memory clicked into place.

A tote bag. That was it! I'd spotted Jody's red tote on her patio, recognized it as being identical to the one I remembered CeCe carrying, and then I'd seen it again tonight at dinner. I'd helped Allison and Phoebe pack up CeCe's room and knew it hadn't been there. But she was never without it.

I forced myself to slow down, to think clearly. I thought back to the night that CeCe had died. She'd entered the lodge sitting room, twirled around greeting people, and searched for the table with the almond drinks. Was she holding anything? No. I was pretty sure she was empty-handed. I closed my eyes. Go farther back in time. She'd entered the sitting room and yes . . . she'd stashed her tote bag in or near the oaken chest beside the door. We all did it; no one would think twice about a bag there.

I jumped up, ready to race over to the lodge. Something important could be in that bag: a note, or information jotted down. A clue as to who would have wanted to snuff out her life. Something. But wait a minute. It was still early. There'd be tons of people around, playing bridge, talking in front of the fire, sipping coffee or tea. Someone in that room might notice me rummaging around in the chest and put it all together. Better wait. Until it's darker and the room's empty.

I did feel a moment of caution and thought briefly about asking Tom or Allison to come with me. But it would be as scary, if not more so, walking up the hill to their villas to ask them, rather than run across the way to the lodge. I'd be really careful. I'd take my flashlight, stay on the lighted paths. It would take only three or four minutes to get there. It was time for me to finish this. *First I'll get the tote,* I decided. *Then I'll tell Nuñez.* In the meantime, I'd wait until midnight.

CHAPTER TWENTY-EIGHT

Later Thursday night

I was so eager to check out my theory about CeCe's red tote bag that I actually found myself pacing the floor of my room, too restless to read, too wired to sit down and go through my article notes. Even as a child I'd had trouble waiting patiently for events to unfold. It wasn't even eight; this was going to be an endless evening. I didn't dare go to the sitting room before midnight, because I knew that the bridge players sometimes hung out there until eleven or later. Or would they tonight, after two deaths at the ranch? Still, I didn't want to take the chance of being seen.

Of course, pacing the floor was healthier than binge eating. As a teenager, I'd dealt with my anxieties and frustrations by buying quarts of mint chocolate chip ice cream and bags of caramels, and methodically working my way through them. That's probably why I kept my refrigerator and pantry so bare here. Luckily, there's no Häagen Dazs store nearby, or even a supermarket, so I'd just keep pacing.

It was only ten forty p.m. in New York. Maybe someone would be in the *MetroScene* office. At least I could leave a message for Dennis. It would give me something productive to do. I grabbed my own tote bag and walked briskly up the hill to the pool area. A rush of adrenaline got me up the last bit with breath to spare. It was only after I had left my casita that it had occurred to me to worry about my solitary climb. It wasn't that

I was in denial . . . then again, maybe I was. I told myself that I shouldn't be wandering around alone, but I'd been determined not to let my fear run me. And by now I'd figured out the security guards' routine. I could see them in the distance at several points on my walk. At least it wasn't totally dark yet. The night was glorious, mild, and crystal clear. The moon was just visible over the uneven peaks of the mountain, and the path to the patio was well lit.

I'd climbed up to the villa pool thinking I'd have more privacy on this remote phone than in the administrative office. I was probably giving it more action than it'd had since its installation. I pulled the phone cord out to its limit and sat in the most public area of the patio. And now, as I looked around me, I could see a few people wandering over to their villas, and the sight of them made me feel much safer.

Of course, as I'd hoped, "editor to the stars" Dennis was still in the office.

"You're not calling to tell me I won't get my article," he said, sounding panicked. "I'm saving space for you!"

"You'll get it. D'you still need pictures?"

"No. We found some fabulous publicity shots from a brochure of the ranch we had in the morgue, and Nardy's wife sent a snapshot of him. What about your friend's husband?"

I gave Dennis Buddy's phone number, but I doubted he'd cooperate. Maybe Allison would have a picture of CeCe; I'd ask in the morning. With some kind of twisted pride, I told Dennis about the assaults on my life and limb.

"Dear heart, much as I want this article, your safety comes first." His voice was hoarse with sincerity.

Sure. Dennis would toss me off the mountain himself if he thought it'd make a better story.

"I hope I made it clear that I want you as part of the story, Nora. First person. From the minute you met these people.

Your take on them, on their relationships, on your own work, on management. The papers are full of third-person and PR stuff. I want your voice."

"You'll get it. But Dennis, if a lawyer named Max Weber calls—you've met him, he used to come to all our parties—please don't tell him about the threats to me . . ."

"He's already called, my dear. He wanted me to fax you and tell you to cease and desist. Of course, I couldn't do that. The pages have already been laid out, the cover lines written. We've put out some promos. What could he have been thinking of?"

Probably how to save my life. I pushed Max out of my mind. Dennis and I spoke a little more about the tone of the article and the details of how and when I would send it, then Dennis promised to call Rose and reassure her of my health and sanity. I sat in the lounge chair for several moments after we'd disconnected, then dialed Max's number, as I'd known I would from the time I left my casita.

No answer. His voice mail picked up, with one of those ubiquitous "I'm either on the phone or unavailable to take your call" messages, so in fact I couldn't be sure if he was out or on the phone.

"It's me. I'm okay. Would have loved to speak with you. I'll try again tomorrow." Then, in a tiny voice I couldn't seem to help, I added, "Miss you."

Okay, I'd done what I could to make connections. And I didn't feel any better.

CHAPTER TWENTY-NINE

Late Thursday night
Back at the casita, I started to get nervous about my projected midnight trip to the lodge. I was starting to feel nibbly, so I heated up my uneaten dinner. It didn't interest me any more now than it had in the dining room, but I went through the motions of chewing and swallowing.

I couldn't put off working on the article too much longer. Washing the dishes, tidying up the room, organizing my notes—it was reassuring to know that my techniques to avoid actually getting down to writing were still in place. I finally pulled out my laptop and sat at the table, my fingers poised over the keyboard, immobilized, as has often been the case, by how to begin.

I knew that once I hit on the perfect first line, the one that would set the tone, everything else would click into place. I played around with a dozen different openings, but most of them were either too cute or too bland. I finally decided to play it straight:

"They came to lose weight, to tone, tighten, and toughen. Seventy-five women and thirty men, almost all attractive, fit, and vigorous. They came for nutritious food, clean air fragrant with flowers and herbs, and some pampering. They did not come for murder. Except one."

I pulled my notepad to my lap and started to do a rough outline. For some reason, notes and outlines worked better for me on paper than on the screen. A hangover from precomputer days, I guess. It went more smoothly than I'd expected: I'd do what Dennis wanted and write from a personal, "here's what I saw and thought" point of view. I went over the notes I'd taken over the last few days, then spread out all the faxes I'd gotten from Max's office and from the magazine. By this time, my table was covered with papers, and I'd had to lay some pages on the floor. Finally, I seemed to catch fire. I pulled together all the material about the group of groups, then about the relationships between the members.

I was so absorbed that I didn't notice the time flying by. When my stomach rumbled, I discovered I'd been working for nearly three hours, and it was eleven twenty p.m. I was now really hungry and picking at my doggie bag dinner just hadn't done it. I stared into my refrigerator and could only come up with two slightly wizened but ripe-looking peaches, the remains of a piece of the local goat cheese, and a few slices of slightly stale ranch bread. Toasted under the oven broiler, the bread tasted nutty and delicious; the fruit and cheese were a perfect accompaniment. Once I'd gotten this damned article written, I'd have to do something about improving my food supply. Culinary consultants weren't supposed to eat like college students.

I washed my snack down with fizzy bottled water and dressed for a sleuth's night out: a black sweatshirt, sneakers, and a navy windbreaker. I took only my keys and a flashlight. I left a light on in my cottage, as well as the outside "night-light." Then, walking quickly and quietly, I headed for the lodge.

There was a nearly full moon now high in the sky, but a few wispy clouds glided by, partly obscuring its brilliance. Just as well. A few of the cottages had lights on behind their hot pink and orange curtains, but most were dark. The day began, of course, with a five thirty a.m. meditation class, and even those guests who skipped that and the yoga that followed usually made the six thirty a.m. walks. The schedule made for early nights.

I suddenly stopped walking and checked to make sure there were no other footsteps, no one following me. Only the faraway barks of coyotes and what might have been owls broke the stillness. I was concentrating so hard, I could even hear the skittering of what might have been lizards across the pathways.

It seemed as though I was the only one on the ranch who was awake. That made me feel a bit trembly. Almost there. I just had to get through this next half hour, and I swore I'd not put myself in danger again. I tried not to breathe too loudly. Between walking fast and terror, I was sure my pounding heart could be heard all over the ranch. I tried to relax by telling myself no one could know what I was doing. I hadn't even told Tom or Allison, whom I totally trusted, and no one else could possibly guess.

When I got to the lodge, it was dark and still. I quietly made my way around to the front door, which was, as I'd felt sure it would be, unlocked. Once inside, I pulled the door nearly shut and paused until my eyes became accustomed to the dark. I felt disoriented, unsure at first as to exactly where I was standing.

There was no oak chest beside the door.

After a moment of panic, I realized that in my anxiety I'd mistaken the door at the end of the building for the main entrance. The trunk must be there, where we'd all gotten into the habit of stashing our bags, jackets, and books as soon as we entered the lodge. I knew that housekeeping checked it only at the end of each week, on Saturday mornings, before everyone left. I spotted the trunk across the floor, ran to it quickly, and opened the lid. As in the best of horror stories, it squeaked, and as I knelt down and prepared to search with my fingertips for the tote, I heard the sound of footsteps. At first, I couldn't move. A night watchman? I thought I'd figured out the timing. I lowered the lid carefully, wincing at the squeaks it made coming down, then tiptoed back and knelt behind one of the huge leather sofas. Then the sound of the main door opening, just a crack. If this were a night watchman, he would surely shine his torch inside the building or turn on the lights if he'd seen me open the door. No one moved.

It was a man. I could tell by his height and shoulder width. And he moved as slowly and stealthily as I had moved. He stepped just inside the door and stood still, probably getting adjusted to the dimness as I had done. I couldn't let him, whoever he was, get too adjusted, or he'd see me, even though I was for the moment out of his range. Maybe he didn't know I was here. Maybe he'd come for his own reasons. Maybe that was wishful thinking.

To my dismay, I could see him turn slightly and pull something out of his pocket. My heart was pounding even harder now; I was sure he could hear it. A flashlight, which he turned on and began slowly and methodically pointing into the dark corners to his left. As the beam of the flashlight continued to peer into the edges of the room, I moved too, crawling, keeping out of range. By the time he and his flashlight were at the far door, where I'd entered the room, I had slipped around to the front of the sofa, still evading the flashlight's invasion. I couldn't see him from my vantage point, but evidently he couldn't see me either. And at least the flashlight's beam let me know where he was.

The light moved to the front door again, and his footsteps followed. When I heard the squeak of the chest lid, I was furious. This had been my idea! Someone must have been following me and heard me open the lid. Shit. He shone the flashlight into the trunk and I thought I could see him pull out—what? I couldn't tell if it was a tote. Actually, I couldn't see if he pulled out anything at all. His back was to me, and with the flashlight in front of him, all I could really see were shadows. He closed the lid, then reached down and picked up something on the floor next to the trunk.

I felt a sick disappointment, almost as sick as I felt when I realized that the dark figure, whose profile was now clearly outlined in the doorway, was Simon Neel. Again, not so simple Simon.

CHAPTER THIRTY

Later Thursday night

I waited, miserable and cold, in the slightly open doorway of the lodge until I could see Simon striding back up the hill to his villa. He hadn't even glanced behind him, but I was sure he knew that I (or someone) had been in the lodge, hiding. I slipped out the side door and made my way quietly back to my casita. I wasn't sure why I was taking such pains. The damage had already been done. I was startled for a moment when a man walked past the bridge to where my room was: a security guard.

Back in my room, I tried to figure out what to do about Simon. And to think about what Simon was going to do about me. What did I really know about him? That he was a startlingly handsome man married to a plain, wealthy young woman. That he had been in a real estate investment deal with CeCe's husband, Buddy, and Alan. Someone had told me—was it Allison? No, it was Alan's widow, Mariana—that the deal had fallen through and that Simon had been very upset. So maybe he'd lost a ton of money. And maybe Jody didn't know. All maybe's. I could understand why Simon might have gotten into a shoving match with Alan last Saturday, but what did CeCe have to do with it? And what could he have been looking for tonight?

Maybe it was a coincidence. Maybe he didn't even know anyone was in the sitting room while he was there. I sighed and pushed my curls back behind my ears. Something suddenly felt wrong: my little finger hurt when I used my hand, really hurt, and I realized that the splint and bandage were gone. The swelling had gone down considerably during the day, but I had ignored the looseness of the bandage. It must have slipped off while I was digging around in the trunk.

I was suddenly sick of conjectures, frightened to think of the consequences of tonight's misadventure. I made sure all the window locks were in place, double-locked the door to the casita, and shoved a chair against the door handle. Then I sat back in front of my laptop. I was too hopped-up to sleep, couldn't bear to think about what would happen tomorrow. Maybe I should go talk to Allison, stay in her villa tonight. But that meant walking up that hill alone, in the dark. I was feeling bold, but not reckless.

Spurred on by my annoyance at having lost my chance to get the tote bag—if it had, indeed, been in the chest—I worked through the night. I wasn't going to be able to reveal the murderer by the time the article was due tomorrow night— rather, tonight—but I could lay out the scene using lots of color and background, describe the players, and float some theories. Goodness knows I had plenty of theories.

Around three thirty a.m., in the middle of stretching my arms to the sky, I heard a soft sound outside the casita. Footsteps. My heart started beating so loudly I was afraid it could be heard through the door. The footsteps stopped. I held my breath, then slipped off my shoes and tiptoed into the kitchen, ducking down as I passed the curtained windows. I'd brought a few pieces of silverware to my room from the staff kitchen, among them a small, serrated knife to cut bread and fruit. I eased open the kitchen drawer and pulled out the knife, then stood still, listening as hard as I could. A distinct thud sounded at my door, then I heard the footsteps receding. I waited for what seemed an eternity, then went back into the main room and sat down at the table. I was shaking so hard I couldn't even put the knife down quietly; it slipped out of my hand onto the tabletop. All was still.

I tried to see outside through the peephole and cautiously peered through the side curtains, but I could see only directly in front of me, not below. No one was there. Knife in hand, I moved the blockade in front of the door and carefully opened it a crack. At my doorstep was a red tote bag. And inside the bag was the splint from my finger.

No way was I able to sleep.

By dawn, I'd managed to finish a rough draft of the article about "death on the spa plan." I was determined to meet tonight's deadline, although I had a noontime class to teach as well as a two-o'clock appointment with Miguel to firm up menu plans for the new week. Would there be a new week? I hadn't heard that there'd been any massive cancellations in the wake of the deaths. It generally took nine months to a year to get a reservation here, and I guess not everyone has my priorities.

Miguel wouldn't take well to postponing our meeting. The article would get done. I worked best under pressure, although this was really pushing it. My intense concentration kept me from obsessing too much more about Simon and about his behavior last night. But I couldn't let it go. Had he followed me to the lodge? And why? I didn't believe that much in coincidence. He couldn't have thought of CeCe's bag at the exact moment I did.

It was five thirty a.m., and I decided to try for a nap. I set the alarm for eight a.m. and crawled into bed, exhausted emotionally as well as physically. One more day. I had terrific regrets about Allison and Tom leaving tomorrow, but along with them would go Simon, Jody, and Phoebe. And maybe a murderer.

A crisp knock at the door awakened me before the alarm. I shuffled to the door. What if it were Simon? What if he wanted to know what I was doing in the lodge last night, what I was writing for the magazine? I didn't know what to do, whether to answer the door or pretend I wasn't home. I stood on my tiptoes to look through the peephole, then shoved the chair out of the way, unlocked and pulled open the door.

"Max! Oh my God, Max." I grabbed hold of him and held on with all my strength, crying his name over and over until he held my face still with both hands and kissed me. It was a kiss worth waiting all these months for. How could I have wondered if I still loved him? Max pulled me closer to him and murmured my name, told me how scared he'd been about my safety, how much he'd missed me. I pulled him farther into the room. He kicked the door closed behind him, then rested his head against mine and just held me.

He pushed me away for a moment, looking at me with intense concern.

"Where's your splint? Your finger can't be healed already," he said hoarsely. "And your throat? Did he choke you?"

I shook my head.

"You know all my little secrets," I said, not really joking. I couldn't quite get myself to smile. "I didn't want you to worry." He didn't say anything, just shook his head in turn.

"I flew to San Diego last night," he said finally, "then rented a car at the airport. I had to wait at the border until it opened. Now I need coffee, and we have to have a long talk." He took off his leather jacket and tossed it on a chair.

"No coffee, honey, I'm sorry. There's tea, I can make Lemon Zinger."

He made a face but moved with me to the kitchen.

"We can go to the dining room for breakfast," I added, "soon as you'd like."

"What I'd like, what I need, is more of you. I've missed you, Nora. More than I thought I would, maybe more than I'm comfortable with."

I didn't know what to say. I was thrilled to see Max, passionately aware of him, but something held me back.

"So you know all about my injuries, hmm?" I said, knowing I was retreating. "Nuñez, right? Damn, he's a motormouth. How did you two guys get together, anyhow?" I was busying myself around the tiny kitchen, boiling water, finding tea bags.

"He'd seen those faxes I'd sent to you, and he knew I had information about your buddies here that he could use. So he called me. It's important that my office maintain good Latin American relations," he added teasingly.

I smiled, still feeling a restraint.

Max was no dummy. He put his arms around me and talked into my hair.

"Are you sorry I came, honey?" he asked softly. "I know you've come here to get away from New York, and me. To start something fresh. I'm proud of what you're doing. I just wish to hell it didn't involve murder. I don't want to interfere, but you had asked for my help and . . ."

"There's a difference between asking for your professional help and needing you to take care of me," I said carefully.

"I needed to be here for my sake. I was worried about you, dammit. Can't you just be glad to see me?"

"I am. I truly am, Max." And I was. And I knew I loved him. But I still felt sad, as if I'd lost something important to me.

CHAPTER THIRTY-ONE

Friday dawn

It felt so wonderfully right to be in each other's arms that our move to the bed was totally natural. Our being apart so many months made me a little awkward at first, but very soon the wonder and excitement of feeling his familiar and much-loved body against mine took over. We made love with passion and intensity, and I didn't want to let go of him when it was over. Didn't want to return to the sparring and struggle for control that had made up so much of our recent relationship.

"You haven't mentioned how much more flexible I am," I finally murmured.

Max laughed, kissed me lightly, then got out of bed and pulled me toward the shower. It was a tiny enclosure, but we stayed too wrapped up together to mind. By the time the hot water had faded to lukewarm, I was boneless.

Max reached for one of the fluffy bath towels. I wrapped myself up in my robe and followed him out of the bathroom.

I found a clean white shirt and some jeans, then hunted through the tangled sheets and coverlet for my socks.

"Hate to criticize your housekeeping, honey, but this place looks like a crime scene."

"I was working all night," I muttered, gathering papers together from the floor, the table, and the chairs. "Here," I said, shoving the printout of the rough draft of my article at him. "Educate yourself while I tidy up. The maid won't know what's garbage and what's to stay." I suddenly remembered the kettle jumping around on the burner and turned off the gas. Too late. The water had evaporated and the bottom of the kettle was burned.

Max was silent as he read the article, occasionally pursing his lips and once sighing deeply. When he was finished, he looked at me thoughtfully.

"Nuñez hadn't mentioned your tea party with the Cerillo brothers," he said finally.

"There's something else I have to tell the inspector," I said, anticipating Max's inevitable reaction. "I, um, had this idea last night, too late to tell him."

Max's response to my tote bag hunt and identification of Simon as the man who had either followed me or second-guessed me seemed mild until I saw a muscle jumping along his jaw.

"Think you're Nancy Drew?"

I smiled tentatively. "More like Brenda Starr, girl reporter."

Neither of us laughed. Finally, Max stood up and stretched.

"Nuñez has all kinds of data about Nardy and his money-laundering minicareer," he said. "The Cerillos think Alan was doing some solo playing, slipping money into a separate account, for him, not for them. They didn't like that, of course, but didn't really know how to get proof of his activities. They're small potatoes, and up to now have only dealt with marijuana. There's been some noise, however, about their being approached by a bigger outfit near Tijuana that's eager to use the ranch and its very strategic location to move cocaine in over the mountains. By the way," he added, neatly stacking up the pages of my article, "Nuñez will have to take a look at these before you send them, to make sure you're not jeopardizing any case he might have. He's much smarter than the Cerillos."

"Wait just a minute, Weber," I said, my voice climbing in instant irritation. "Just because I'm besotted by you and thrilled you've been worrying about me doesn't mean you get to come in and tell me what to do."

Max grinned. "Besotted, eh?"

"I'm not showing my article to Inspector Nuñez like a good little girl."

"Even if it means you'll screw up his chances to get evidence of who killed Nardy and your little friend?"

"And how come you know all that stuff about the Cerillos, and the drug trade, and the accounts? I'm not grown-up enough for Nuñez to have told this stuff to? Or I'm the wrong gender?"

I whirled around, wanting to throw something, but settled on pulling on my jacket. Okay for him to be told I was besotted, he seemed to like that, but has he told me he loved me? Has he even commented on how much weight I'd lost? How much more fit I looked? Just came in here, took over my body and now my work. I felt closed in, an old, familiar feeling.

"I've got a class to prepare for at noon, then a meeting with my chef. I have to finish the article by this afternoon, so if you and your inspector buddy have comments, they'll have to be made by two-thirty, in time for me to incorporate any changes and send it off to New York."

Max nodded his head.

"I'll find the inspector and set up a meeting while you teach your class. But I need something to eat."

I nodded and tied up my sneakers. While Max finished getting dressed, I filled my tote bag with my class plan and notes for the kitchen staff, then we went off to scrounge up some food. How quickly our passionate reunion became an old scenario, with Max tight-lipped and irritated and me feeling diminished and controlled.

CHAPTER THIRTY-TWO

Friday, early morning

Miguel, despite his recent aloofness, was so excited to meet my *amigo* from New York that he embraced Max in a bear hug. Miguel had been worrying about me since I'd arrived, unable to accept that I was unmarried, unattached, and unconcerned. Little did he know. I fixed myself a cup of tea, helped myself to some cereal, and sat at my desk in a corner of the kitchen. I'd let Miguel feed Max while I decided what to say to the group leaving the ranch.

The talk on this last full day was usually called "adapting the ranch at home," but I was afraid that what the departing guests would really take home would be gossip and horror at the double murders. I'd have to work a little harder to focus their minds on changing their food habits.

Whenever I lifted my head from recipes and calorie counts, I could hear Miguel and Max laughing about *huevos rancheros*. I was impressed. Miguel's version of the classic Mexican home-style breakfast had as much to do with chopped potatoes, peppers, onions, sharp cheese, chilies, and salsa as it did with eggs. Max wasn't usually—or hadn't been in the past—so adventurous about food. I watched warily as he thanked Miguel, grabbed a peach from the baskets of fresh fruit beside the counter, and came over to where I was sitting.

"It's your article, honey," he said softly. "Let me just be here for you. I promised Nuñez I'd look him up this morning.

Remember I'm on your side." He kissed me and took off. Miguel beamed at both of us.

By the time Miguel and I had worked through next week's menu (I was adding a spicy pumpkin soup and meltingly good cinnamon applesauce—in tiny portions of course—among other fall treats), and I'd sampled some of the soup along with a healthy portion of nutty seven-grain ranch bread, it was almost time for my talk to the departing guests. I never knew from week to week how many to expect. Today I thought there'd be at least a dozen. My theory was that no one wanted to hang around on their own on this last day before they went home.

I photocopied the standard "low-fat, low-sugar" instruction sheets, tips about portion control and defensive shopping, and eight recipes, then assembled my handouts and walked over to the shaded patio beside the main pool. There was no use pretending the ranch was not under siege. Uniformed police were everywhere, watching, talking to guests and making notes, talking to one another. One of the cooks had told me that they'd all been interviewed twice, and Miguel had complained bitterly about the violation to his kitchen. Every item had been examined, samples of soups sent to a lab, ingredients for the liquid fast program confiscated. All eminently sensible steps, but chilling and necessary reminders that, despite my professional concerns and the resumption of what might be a love life, murder had been committed here.

I had underestimated the guests' anxiety or their wish to hold on to the part of the ranch experience they'd enjoyed. There were at least two dozen women and men waiting for me. I rushed back to the kitchen and asked one of the kitchen aides to photocopy more pages, then went again to the patio and sat among the guests, congratulating some on their weight loss and giving a pep talk to those who were disappointed. It was impossible to avoid discussing Alan's and CeCe's deaths, but I knew they'd already gone over them endlessly.

In an attempt to distract them, I described how years ago, the ranch nutritionist had weighed and measured each guest as they arrived on a Saturday and recommended a specific number of calories for them to ingest each day. The calories were, and still are, marked clearly on little signs at the breakfast and lunch buffets, and on the table menus at dinner. The guests were also weighed and measured on their last day. It was only a few years ago that the nutrition staff realized the emphasis was askew. People were fixated on how many calories they were eating, how much weight they'd lost, and what their measurements were rather than on what sorts of food to eat for nutritious, balanced meals, and what kind of exercise would work best for them.

Today, I explained, we encourage balanced choices, modest portions of all the food we offer. The diet usually totals about eleven hundred calories a day. But there were also cereals available at breakfast, sweetened and unsweetened fresh lemonade all day, treats for those (like Allison) who were almost too thin and needed the occasional burrito or guacamole dip. Actually, I pointed out, no one monitored you here. We assume everyone's a grown-up. Anyone could ask for extra portions, and more than a few, especially the men, do.

Maybe because I was a food writer and not a nutritionist, we always had fun at this session. I'd keep it light and upbeat. But today everyone was uptight and polite. No hugs, few expressions of appreciation from those who'd attended my talks and cooking classes. Small wonder, but a bit of a letdown.

Walking back to my casita, I noticed Allison sunbathing by the pool. I wasn't the only one who noticed her. Three local policemen faced the pool, their mirrored sunglasses pointed in her direction. Allison's lush, bikini-clad body had turned a warm, toasty color, and at first I thought her asleep. As I paused near her lounge chair, however, she opened one eye and growled, "Now that your honey is here, you're going to pass me by?"

I laughed and sat on an adjacent lounge chair.

"Word sure gets around fast. I want you to meet him, Allison. Shall I bring him to dinner tonight? That's if I finish my article in time, and he and I are still speaking."

"Dinner isn't until eight thirty, so you should be able to make it. Fight on your own time. You'll have to have your margaritas at the restaurant. The rest of us are meeting earlier at my place. Cindy and Joey, from the fitness staff, are joining us. We're going to Carmelita's," she added, waving vaguely in the direction of the highway, "about three miles north. Over that hill where we hear the grinding of truck gears all night."

"Will they let us leave the ranch do you think?"

"They'll have to—lots of folk going home tonight, not even waiting for the morning. There've been lawyers from San Diego, an attaché from the American embassy in Mexico City, all sorts of big guns."

She raised the back of her chair and put on her sunglasses.

"What's Nuñez been saying? Coming up with any answers?"

"Be damned if I know. I did a real stupid thing last night, could have gotten myself in serious trouble. But I thought maybe CeCe's tote bag would still be in the chest, you know, in the lodge. And it might have a clue as to what she was so eager to talk to me about. Someone grabbed it before I could get to it. Least I think he got it. Scared me to death." I hesitated, then plunged ahead. "It was Simon."

"Was it now?" she murmured.

I couldn't see her eyes, just the sunglasses reflecting back a troubled me.

"Well," she said finally, "maybe there was stuff in the bag about the new town Buddy was planning that Alan and Simon had invested in. CeCe seemed like a bubblehead, but she knew everything Buddy was doing. Maybe Simon thought it could incriminate him." She smiled wickedly. "You can ask him at dinner tonight."

"Great. Thanks a lot. Gotta go. I'm meeting with the detective soul mates of the new millennium. They found each other, joined in a mutual concern that I will put my feet squarely in their case."

I continued on my way home, excited to see Max. Despite my misgivings about our relationship. What had he been up to these last few hours? Had he been enjoying the scenery, particularly that of firm young female bodies?

As I approached the casita, I could hear Phoebe's throaty laugh. She'd sure as hell never visited me before. Max was sitting on the bench on my deck, leaning back against the rail.

"Share the joke, guys?"

"Oh," said Phoebe airily, "we were just exchanging gossip about some people we know in common. We can continue at dinner tonight, Max. See you then."

Without even saying good-bye to me, she sauntered off.

"Didn't take you long, Weber."

He smiled at me so sweetly I felt myself smiling back. "She's certainly a pistol. Loaded for bear. But I don't think she knows much. Doesn't even really know, but maybe suspects, that her skinny boyfriend spreads dope around." He stood up beside me and rubbed my shoulders.

"You look tired, about as tired as I feel. Wanna take a nap?" He wiggled his eyebrows à la Groucho Marx.

"What about Nuñez?"

"I told him your sad story. He wasn't too happy but seemed to accept your interference philosophically. He's on his way to talk to Simon. Not just about the tote bag, I gather."

He pulled me into his arms and I felt myself relax, tucking

my head cozily under his chin. Then I yawned.

Max laughed. "I won't take it personally. We've both had too little sleep."

"You sleep. I need to edit my article, puff it out a bit. Then I'll give it a rest, take a last look just before dinner. I'll send it out as an e-mail attachment, using the line at the front desk."

"I'm not going to fight you on this one, honey. I've got to close my eyes. But although I kept Nuñez off your back, I'd like to check your piece for libel before you send it on to New York."

I pulled back from his embrace. "Thank you so much for the vote of confidence, Mr. United States Attorney."

"Give it a rest, Nora. I haven't interfered, and I don't want to, but someone's got to check . . ."

"Let's leave that to the magazine's lawyers, Max. That's what they're paid for. I appreciate your concern for my safety and for my journalistic accuracy, but I'd rather we keep our relationship . . ."

"Remember your call to me on Monday? You asked for my help then, as I recall. And I sent you a ream of information. Stuff it would take you weeks to find out on your own. Seems to me you're pretty arbitrary about when and how you want my help."

I didn't respond. Couldn't. He was right. His information had been enormously helpful, but I didn't want him to help anymore.

CHAPTER THIRTY-THREE

Later Friday afternoon

I was exhausted and I couldn't stay focused. I knew I'd think more clearly if I were rested. I set my internal alarm clock and slept for a couple of hours, then slipped out of bed, leaving Max still zonked. I looked at him for a long time. He looked so dear to me. Why did we have to butt heads all the time? It was all too easy to blame him. He is autocratic and instructive and needs to be right all the time. But, then, so do I.

I forced myself to sit down at my computer and take one last look at the article for *MetroScene*. By now, I was sick of it. I'd spent days obsessing about it, to what end? Nearly three thousand words of color and conjecture. Some facts. Well, the words weren't bad. And the facts, those I had, were solid. While no one was going to be able to indict on the basis of this article, I'd given a clear, personal, and if I dare say so, richly textured picture of the ranch and its activities, the guests and staff, and the two deaths. I'd followed Dennis's instructions that I "put myself into it," and included a somewhat dramatic account of my "accidents." I'd even laid out the cases against Simon or Jody (I liked that touch, adding Jody as a suspect), Joe, and the Cerillos—all in the most subtle and elliptical way, of course.

I wasn't entirely naive. I knew that the magazine's lawyers would be up pretty late tonight, checking and rechecking my allusions, hints, character sketches. I would tell *MetroScene* to get the background material from Max's office.

One step at a time. I left a note for Max saying where I was going and that I'd be back by six thirty, and walked briskly toward the administration building with my laptop and the background material from the U.S. Attorney's office in my tote.

There seemed to be even more of the private security guards and policemen stationed around the grounds than earlier in the day. Nuñez obviously didn't want anyone leaving unannounced. Maybe he wanted to give reassurance to the remaining guests. Whatever his motive, it felt as though we were under siege. None of the uniformed men met my eyes. Actually, none of the dozen or so guests I saw met my eyes either. I think they were all eager to get out of here, get away from tragedy. From the threat of further tragedy.

For the first time, I let myself wonder what the long-term effect would be on the ranch. I assumed that out there in the real world, there were public relations agents working their magic, spinning their spin. I'd been totally self-absorbed, thinking only of myself and the few people whose motives and actions interested me.

As I neared the steps of the administration building, I sensed someone approaching me on my left, moving in too close and too quickly for my comfort. I turned and almost bumped into Christian Benedine, looking today much more like a hit man than the ranch marketing director he purported to be. He had on a gray T-shirt tucked into black sweatpants, and his black running shoes and baseball cap reinforced the cliché. Dark sunglasses, the kind that seemed to shimmer with color, completed the picture. Lots of muscle was revealed, not much else. I took a few steps away from him.

"Ms. Franke, how good to see you. You saved me a trip to your room. I'm so glad I didn't have to disturb you and your boyfriend."

"Call me Nora," I said automatically. His lips curved slightly.

"We're not friends, Ms. Franke. Shall we go into the office?" he asked and, not waiting for an answer, took my elbow and propelled me up the stairs.

"I don't need your help in walking," I said as I tried to shake off his hand.

He gripped my elbow even more firmly and directed me behind the reservations desk toward the small room where we'd talked before. I held on tightly to my laptop and tote, still resisting his pull, but I didn't bother trying to get help from the young girl behind the counter. She was staring at us as if spellbound, but I knew her loyalty would be to Benedine, not to myself.

The office was as claustrophobic as I'd remembered, and this time Christian closed and locked the door firmly.

"Victor Cerillo is very disappointed in you, Ms. Franke." He spoke coldly and, as usual, without animation. "He's been in Tijuana today, meeting with his lawyer, but he's anxious to speak to you. I'll pick you up here, tomorrow, ten a.m."

I nodded and sat down before my knees could give out. I cleared my throat and tried to sound calm.

"Will it take long, Christian? I'd figured on working all day to catch up with my plans for next week . . ."

Christian smiled, without humor. "I don't think you have to worry about next week, Ms. Franke."

My heart started pounding. I was sure he could hear it. "What do you mean? Are you threatening me?"

"Certainly not. As long as you do the right thing, you have nothing to worry about."

"I don't understand. What do you mean, 'do the right thing'? That sounds like a line from the movies."

"I think you understand, Ms. Franke." Christian stood, and I flinched reflexively.

"You're very tense. Look how you're clutching that computer.

I'll be happy to relieve you of its weight." He walked around the edge of the desk and took the laptop away from my firm grip as if it weighed ounces rather than pounds.

"You won't need this right now," he said.

"I've already sent the article," I lied. "What's in the computer won't do you any good." Shit. Dennis was always warning reporters to lock their documents. But who'd ever wanted to get into my restaurant reviews? "And that laptop cost more than a thousand dollars. I want it back."

"You'll get it back. When we've read the article." He scowled. "When is it due?"

"Today," I said with bravado.

"You'll have to stop its publication."

"I can't," I said, lying again, but now, finally, getting panicky. "Once they get it, it goes directly into production."

Maybe he wouldn't know that that, too, was a lie. First Dennis will pore over the article, then my researcher, Wendy, will check whatever facts she can access, then layout will add whatever photographs they came up with, then the lawyers, who'd start reviewing it from the minute it came over the wires, would make their changes, then . . . unless I get this damned piece to them tonight, it will never make Sunday's deadline. And it was obvious that I couldn't use the phone lines here to e-mail the story to New York.

"Why hasn't Victor badgered me about the magazine article before?" I challenged him. "It was stupid not to. Didn't you or he know I'd be sending it in today?"

"How should we know? We thought it was some kind of monthly magazine, that you'd be working on it for weeks. Why would we know?"

Why indeed? I'd been thinking I was dealing with a big-time Mafialike operation, when the truth was, Victor and his partners were ambitious but unsophisticated small-time ranchers.

Christian was still scowling, clearly uncomfortable with the knowledge that he—and the Cerillos—were out of their depth.

"Let me see that bag," he said finally, pointing to the tote bag I was still clutching. I held onto the bag.

"Victor's seen all this material," I said, hating the conciliatory tone in my voice. "It's the background material the U.S. Attorney's office faxed to me here," I added, hoping to impress him with my supposed importance.

He leaned over the desk and pulled the tote from my hands, shuffled through the papers, then tossed the bag back to me.

"Your boyfriend's office," he muttered, putting me in my place. "You amateurs. Messing around with stuff you don't know about. You're almost as bad as Nardy was. Thinking you're smarter than us. You're trying to bring us down. Maybe not the way he tried to, but . . ."

"How did he try to?"

Christian couldn't seem to resist showing off his knowledge of the inner circle.

"Well, I know Victor told you Nardy was investing the money for us, whatever money we didn't take care of here." And his arm swept around, indicating, I assumed, the ranch as a whole.

"Laundering," I said.

Christian raised an eyebrow. "Reinvesting. He got a nice cut for his work. Greedy bastard. Wasn't enough for him. Set up his own account. Sort of a business inside the business." He gave a short imitation of a laugh. "Didn't think he was smart enough, or ballsy enough, to try it, tell you the truth. Victor'd asked him for an accounting, y'know. All sorts of shit was hitting the fan. Someone saved us the trouble of ending his career."

I was stunned. Maybe Victor did get into a fight with Alan; maybe he left him to die on the mountain. But why CeCe? And how? The Cerillos never hung around the ranch. Alan must have had an accomplice. Had to be Simon. I couldn't believe, any more than Christian did, that the Alan I'd heard about had the smarts—or guts—to double-cross his brothers-in-law. My head was spinning; I'd have to figure out how to use this new tidbit.

Christian woke up from his reverie and brusquely motioned me out of the room.

"Tomorrow morning. Ten a.m. Be here." He followed me to the door, and I heard the lock turn behind me.

I waited at the side of the entrance foyer until my breathing steadied and I thought my legs would carry me, then I hurried toward the three phone booths at the end of the lobby. I entered the end one and placed a call to *MetroScene*. It seemed an endless procedure. First, the switchboard here had to get the long-distance operator. Then the Mexican operator asked me to hang up and promised she'd call me back as soon as she had a connection. When she did, and I heard the magazine's switchboard operator, I let out a sigh of relief. I asked to be connected to Dennis, heard him say, "Hello," then the line went dead. I kept calling Dennis's name, but there was that heavy, almost palpable silence that spoke of empty air. Well, this was Mexico, after all. I tried again, but this time the operator said she couldn't get through at all.

Whether it was the Mexican or Cerillo telephone system, I figured I might as well give up for now, from this phone. We'd already checked Max's cellular phone, to no avail. The mountains interfered too much. I walked through the entrance foyer of the administration building and passed a small table topped by a basket labeled "Lost and Found." There, as if in a final insult to my pride, lay my bright red tote bag, totally empty.

CHAPTER THIRTY-FOUR

Early Friday evening

It was dark by the time I walked down the steps and headed back to the casita. The presence of all the policemen should have calmed any residual anxieties I had about my safety, but I felt only numb. I should have felt relieved If the Cerillos or Tamayo had been responsible for my "accidents," then now that the article was supposedly submitted there was no further need to warn me off. But what if it wasn't them I should be worried about?

As I crossed the little bridge to where the staff quarters were, I saw Max walking quickly toward me. I ran to meet him and flew into his arms. After uttering an "umph" from the impact of my tote bag on his back, he held me tight.

"Tell me," he said.

The words just spilled out of me, my voice shaking with anger and not a little fear. "I couldn't send the article. Christian met me there, threatened me. He took my laptop so they can read what I wrote. I told him I'd sent it in already but I'm not sure he believed me. Now I have to meet with Victor in the morning. He's going to fire me. I just know it."

Max started to laugh. "Well, of course he's going to fire you, you ninny. What did you expect?"

It took me a minute, but then I started to laugh too.

"Just because I'm hinting in print, to tens of thousands of readers, that Victor Cerillo or his brother might be a murderer?

And that they might be drug traffickers? For that he's going to fire me? What about my great recipes? And my cookbook ideas? And all the weight I still have to lose?"

By this time I was laughing hysterically. Max just held me, grinning, while I continued to giggle. When I had finally wound down, Max asked, "How much time do you think we have before we have to get out of town, Kimosabe?"

"He'll probably throw me out tomorrow." Now I had the hiccups. "We can take the first plane out we can make. I sure as hell can't use their phone lines to e-mail the damned article, and I need to get it to the magazine tonight. Thank God I've got it saved on a disk." I thought about it for a moment, still hiccuping. "How good's your relationship with Nuñez?"

"Good enough. Let's go back and change for dinner. We have time to stop by his office, but I'm afraid now you'll have to show him the article."

I nodded resignedly. So much for my bravado in not showing it to him earlier. Keep focused, Franke. The article's finished. And you're not. Yet.

CHAPTER THIRTY-FIVE

Friday night

Max had called ahead, so Inspector Nuñez was waiting for us in the municipal police office when we got there at seven. He greeted us as politely as always, showing a bit more warmth to Max than to me, but then, Max had been more cooperative with him.

"I need a favor from you, Inspector, and in return I'll tell you what I learned this afternoon." Out of the corner of my eye, I could see Max wince at the arrogance implicit in my offer. It was too late to restate my offer, but fortunately Nuñez looked amused rather than angry.

"By all means, *Señorita* Nora, let us exchange favors. What is it that you need?"

"Could I try to find a computer program here that's compatible with mine so I can print the article I wrote? I've got a disk." When Nuñez raised his eyebrows in an unspoken query, I added, "Victor Cerillo's henchman took my computer from me before I could e-mail the article to my magazine."

He took me by the arm and with great patience and courtesy walked me through the busy office until we found an administrator who had the Microsoft Word program I used, and stood with me as my article spewed out of the shared printer. I then handed the pages to him with a small bow, and he led Max and me into a spacious, well-lit office. He read and reread the article. He clucked his tongue a few hundred times, and commented that *MetroScene*'s lawyers would certainly be busy. But nothing in the piece seemed to surprise or alarm him, so I decided I'd been on target. Either that or I'd missed it entirely.

"This afternoon I learned that Alan Nardy was playing his own game," I offered. "He evidently set up his own account, apart from that for the Cerillos."

Nuñez continued to look serene, nodding his head calmly.

"This isn't news to you, is it?" I asked, let down.

He smiled and shook his head. "But I appreciate your coming to me with what you've learned."

"May I use this desk to e-mail my material?"

He nodded his head this time and waved me toward the computer.

When I'd finished, I found Nuñez and Max discussing rules of evidence in the U.S. and Mexico. He wouldn't tell me whether an arrest was imminent or whether any of the suspects would be detained before they all left tomorrow. Just that everything was being taken care of. He was one step away from patting me on the head and telling me not to worry my sweet little self. He did say he'd look for us at lunchtime.

No one except Allison, and maybe Phoebe, who was intrigued by Max, seemed particularly thrilled to see us when we finally showed up at Carmelita's. I wasn't sure why I'd agreed to meet for a farewell dinner with what remained of the embarrassingly named "posse." It wasn't as though I'd miss most of them. Phoebe was as brittle and clever as usual, while Joey sat glowering at me. Simon was off somewhere in his head; and Jody looked as if she were about to cry. It was Tom I was glad to see, and yet I felt really bad about him. He looked lonely, and I felt guilty as hell, although I'd been straight with him. Hadn't I?

Max wasn't totally insensitive to the awkwardness between Tom and me. He swiveled his head between us more than once as Tom and Allison and I chattered about other guests and wondered how badly the ranch would be hurt by the double murders and the attendant publicity. Phoebe pointed out that my writing an article would help fan the fires, and I calmly agreed. When I announced that I expected to be fired by the ranch owners, no one seemed terribly surprised.

"We've been expecting you to be asked to leave before now," said Cindy, the altogether too chirpy young aerobics instructor Phoebe and Allison had invited to dinner. "After all, Dolores told everyone you were writing an article for a fancy New York City magazine and would be telling gossip and stuff about the ranch."

"I don't write gossip," I said with irritation. Max kicked me under the table, and I let it pass.

"Who's going to fire you?" asked Allison. "Dolores?"

I shook my head, hesitant to reveal the owners of the ranch, even though my article doing so would, with any luck, be out next week.

"So, did you solve the crimes, Nora the frank?" Simon was definitely drunk. He'd skipped the margaritas, sangrias, and Tecate beer and gone straight, and often, to Scotch.

"No one's been arrested yet," I answered blithely. "Anyway, this isn't one of those Agatha Christie stories, where everyone gathers together in one place and the murderer is revealed."

Allison laughed. "What a shame! It would make this a truly memorable meal. Now we just have to rely on the drinks and the food. No offense, Nora, but this chicken mole is too incredible for words after an abstentious week. And the rice and beans don't taste at all like yours."

"It's the fat, guys. As those in the business say, 'fat makes fat.' Of course, it also makes everything taste great. Guess I wasn't right for a spa kitchen, after all."

"What'll you do now?" asked Cindy with a bit too much

sympathy to believe. "Will you be, like, broke?"

"I'll keep on reviewing restaurants and maybe write a spa cookbook of my own." I'd just thought of that. "I might be able to find another spa connection. Not to worry."

"Who'd worry about you?" asked Jody spitefully. "You sure as heck didn't worry about spoiling any of our lives."

And that was the high point of the dinner.

"I'm holding you to your promise to climb the mountain with all of us in the morning," said Allison. "We'll go on up right behind the meditation hike, 'round about six fifteen. That way you won't have to worry about delaying anyone behind us, and we can all talk as much as we like."

I nodded my agreement, and Max said he'd come, too. If I promised to return his car in San Diego when I left, so he wouldn't have to drive to the airport in the morning and could instead take the ranch van.

"Okay," I decided. "Might as well leave here achieving one of my goals. Long as I can make a ten-o'clock appointment."

Allison laughed. "You'll be back for the eight thirty breakfast," she promised.

Max and I said our good nights while the others were still nibbling away on flan and meringues with whipped cream and fruit. I was exhausted. I hadn't really caught up on the sleep I'd lost, and I was emotionally drained from my meeting with Christian. If I was going to climb Mount Cuchuma at dawn, however slowly, I was going to need all the sleep I could get.

CHAPTER THIRTY-SIX

Saturday morning

I couldn't believe I was actually getting up at five thirty a.m., after a night of margaritas. I'd been so tired that I'd left my contact lenses in overnight, and my eyes felt full of sand. Since none of us had phones in our rooms, there was no way I could reach Allison to beg off my promise to hike the mountain. And despite the warm afterglow of our lovemaking when we got back to my casita last night, Max had denied he'd ever agreed to accompany me up the mountain. He said he'd take his own walk, thank you very much, on a flat surface. Later in the morning.

I was feeling ridiculously stressed. Somehow after the hike I'd have to find the time to shower, change into businesslike clothes, and be ready to meet with Victor Cerillo. If he fired me, as I assumed he would, I intended to leave immediately. I'd have to collect my notes and materials from my desk in the kitchen, pack up my personal belongings, and say good-bye to Miguel and the few other staff people I liked. I assumed I'd have to have another interview with Inspector Nuñez, then I'd drive Max's rental car to San Diego in time to make the last daytime plane to New York. He was planning to take an earlier ranch bus to the airport. I was exhausted just thinking about it. And once in New York, where would I go? My apartment was sublet. Absolutely not my mother's. Maybe Judith. Or Max . . .

I'd miss the ranch. But I'd never really bonded with anyone.

Just a few guests, like poor CeCe, and Allison and Tom. And once Tom saw me with Max at the restaurant last night, that flirtation needed antifreeze.

I pulled back one of the curtains from a side window so I wouldn't need to turn on the light and wake Max, and put on my clothes in the semidarkness. I dressed as though I were going skiing: layers were the answer to the predawn cold and the heat I expected to be generated by exertion. By the time I pulled on my windbreaker, I felt (and undoubtedly looked) like a stuffed animal.

The night-lights on the grounds were still lit, and I could see two security guards talking at the end of the path nearest my casita. They and the others I saw on the way gave me the confidence to walk alone to the clearing where I was to meet Allison and her "posse."

There were quite a few guests there, perhaps as many as thirty, ready for the meditation hike. Some had already started up the trail at the foot of the mountain, walking at their own pace. I was a few minutes early, so I watched Elaine, the astringent head of the hiking program, demonstrate the stretches she wanted everyone to do. No one was talking. It was eerily still. I stretched along with the others, feeling stiff in the early morning cold and envying the flexibility of most of the participants, including Phoebe and Jody. Simon and Tom were there too, moving with more athleticism than grace.

After about ten minutes, Elaine motioned everyone to follow her. I noticed Cindy was the "shepherd" of the hike, staying at the back to make sure no one made a wrong turn or ran into trouble. She waved to me and swung in behind the row of stragglers.

Allison had arrived while I was stretching, and was working on her calf muscles and hamstrings.

"Excited?" she asked teasingly.

"Absolutely. And nervous about climbing. But it's something I've wanted to do since I got here. Just don't laugh at me if I gasp a lot. Or mind if I hold you up."

"I'm not in a rush, lamb. And I'll only laugh with you, not at you." She hitched her knapsack onto her back. "Let's give them another few minutes to get ahead so we won't disturb them by talking. The rest of the gang'll be waiting at the first rise. Where's Max?"

"He decided to sleep in."

I tightened my fanny pack. I was as ready as I'd ever be.

"I'd have thought that Nuñez and company would worry about all of their suspects going up and over a mountain."

Allison shrugged. "Where would we go? It's not as if this is right at the border. And no one's carrying a suitcase."

I smiled, picturing my oversized duffel-on-wheels careening over the rocky path.

We walked slowly through the clearing. The only good thing about my anxiety at making the climb is that it was keeping me from thinking too much about the murderer (surely no one would attack me while I was hiking with a group) and my upcoming interview with Victor Cerillo. We didn't talk much initially as we walked. Allison seemed deep in thought, and not happy thought at that. When I commented on her mood, she said quietly, "It's always hard to leave the ranch, harder than usual this time. I do believe it'll be the last time I come. I guess nothing ever stays the same, and with Alan and CeCe gone . . ."

"Allison," I asked impulsively, "do you know who killed them?"

"Stay out of it now, Nora. I don't want you to be hurt. I've gotten right fond of you this week. Now that your article's done, let it be."

I'd gotten right fond of Allison, too. Amazing, really, since I'd known her for only a week, albeit in a "we're-all-trapped-in-a-lifeboat" situation. But I struggled against her denial.

"How can either of us let it be? Do you want the person who killed your friends to go free, to be unpunished? I can't live with that, and I hardly knew CeCe."

"Oh, I don't think they'll be unpunished, lamb. There's all kinds of punishment." Allison reached for my hand and pulled me across a narrow, muddy ditch as we began our ascent. I could see Tom and Phoebe waiting ahead. Simon and Jody were already out of sight.

"Here we go," she sang out. "Keep up a slow, steady rhythm. You're taking too big steps. Make them shorter. No hurry now. Just keep chugging along."

I tried to follow her example, but couldn't answer. I was already struggling for breath. Not a good sign.

"Clasp your hands behind your back, Nora. Stand up real straight. That way you'll get more oxygen into your lungs."

I was wearing so many upper layers that it wasn't that easy to grasp my hands behind my back, but the effort was worth it. It forced my shoulders back and my chest up. I could actually feel more air getting into my lungs.

We climbed silently for a while, and I felt some of my tension ease. The visibility was improving as the sky lightened, and I was surer of my footing.

"Okay, you win. I just can't keep away from the subject. What do you think's going to happen?" Allison asked. "You must have gotten a hint or two from that enigmatic inspector. You met with him last night before dinner, didn't you?"

"Yeah, Max and I both did. And he told us zilch. He did read my article, though, and I'd like to think that if I were totally off base he'd have said something."

"You didn't actually name names, did you?"

"No, no, of course not. Not this side of libel laws." I spoke very quietly, not sure just how far ahead Simon and Tom were. "I did hint that one of Alan's buddies—and I described Simon pretty clearly, without using his name or saying where he's from—who had invested with him and lost his money might have had reason to fight with him. You know, it did occur to me that Alan's death could have been accidental, at first anyhow. But then, once he was left on the mountain overnight . . . that's a different story."

"And CeCe?"

"She was probably a victim by happenstance. She must have seen something, or learned something, that linked the killer to Alan. Again, I'm betting on Simon. Although," I added, puffing audibly now, "I did mention the Cerillos' name. Figured it was public record, although not talked about. Let the lawyers tell me not to."

"Alan's brothers-in-law? What about them?"

I nodded, trying to save my breath for breathing. Allison turned around on the path ahead of me to see my response. She looked interested but not surprised.

"You know, they're the owners of the ranch," I said.

She nodded. "Alan told me once. What on earth . . . Hell 'n' damn!"

She leaned over and rubbed her left shin, looking up the mountain. Rocks, some pretty big ones, had evidently come loose and were rolling toward us. We were standing directly in their path and had to move briskly to get out of the way. I wasn't hit, but stood stark still, scared and trembly.

"Where did they come from?" I asked a little wildly. The others in our group were ahead of us but out of sight now. I knew there were numerous paths up and around the sides of the mountain, and I wasn't sure which way the others on the meditation hike had gone. Or, for that matter, which way we were going.

Allison used a soothing voice, one I suspected she used with her horse.

"Someone up ahead must have accidentally dislodged them," she said calmly, still rubbing her shin. "It's been real dry. It happens."

I tried to do calming yoga breathing. Although that only worked for me when I was already calm. I pulled my bottle of water out of my fanny pack and took a big gulp. Allison shook her head when I offered her some.

"Will you be okay to continue climbing?" I asked, not sure what I wanted her answer to be.

"Oh sure," said Allison. "Just give me another minute or two."

We sat on boulders on opposite sides of the path and caught our breaths. I figured we were more than halfway up the mountain face. It was so quiet that I could hear the leaves rustle. The birds hadn't begun to sing yet, the sky was still fairly dim, but in the incredibly tender quiet I was intensely aware of fragrances: the spicy aroma of sage, the heavy sweetness of honeysuckle, the light fragrance of bougainvilleas. Never have I experienced such a poignant silence. I wanted it to go on forever. As long as no one kicked any more rocks down at us.

"I'm okay now," said Allison abruptly. "Ready to roll. I'd like to catch up with the gang before they get worried and come back looking for us. Distract me now. What were you saying about the Cerillos?"

I thought about it for a moment as we resumed climbing. "Well, you said you knew that they were the owners of the ranch. Alan was laundering their funny money for them. Carried it across the border in his gym bag probably. He must've invested some back into the ranch, but into other businesses as well. I heard he stashed a lot away somewhere to help the Cerillos avoid taxes and keep the Feds and Mexican tax officials from wondering how come the ranch is so profitable. I gather he was siphoning some off to his own accounts."

"Tucked away on the Cayman Islands," said Allison absently.

I stopped climbing. "How do you know that? Did he tell you?"

Allison nodded. "Nuñez knows. He asked me if I knew. Wanted to know how much Alan shared with me. Fact is, Alan couldn't keep his mouth shut. He probably told CeCe too. And heaven knows who else."

"What is it about the Cayman Islands? I'm not sure I even know where they are."

"The Caribbean. Beaches are okay, nothing special. Some glitzy hotels. Before they established the island as a tax haven, with Swiss-type laws of confidentiality, they were famous for their turtle farms."

I laughed, thinking she was kidding, but she looked totally serious. I stopped in the path again and shuffled around uncomfortably.

"Allison, I've been trying to ignore this, but . . . I need to pee in the worst way. And I'd rather do it before we catch up with everyone."

She grinned. "You looking for indoor plumbing, perhaps, with hot and cold running water? See the chaparral over there? Those short, stocky shrubs?"

"I was hoping for more cover."

"There's your outhouse, Nora Franke. Got any tissues?"

I nodded, wondering if I could tough it out. No, I'd never make it to the next landing, much less back down the mountain. It had been a catch-22: I'd needed to chug water while climbing and sweating, but the water meant I couldn't climb any farther without making a pit stop.

As I hesitated at the side of the mountain path, Allison grinning at me from a few feet above, I looked back over the edge of the mountain to the valley below. In the predawn light, Rancho de las Flores looked like a misty impressionist painting, a grayish-green oasis in the stark Sierra Madre landscape of granite rocks and boulders. Neat rows of vineyards laden with fat grapes could be dimly seen, with feathery olive trees shining silver in the wind. The ranch seemed at peace with the landscape. I was going to miss this. For its beauty and its serenity. But now the serenity was gone, wasn't it?

CHAPTER THIRTY-SEVEN

Later Saturday morning

I felt foolish being such a wimp. I moved purposefully toward the shrubs while Allison looked tactfully away. In the utter stillness I could hear the murmur of voices. They could be stragglers from the meditation hike ahead, breaking their vow of silence. But as I emerged from my hideout, yanking in place the layers of clothing I'd worn, I heard a woman's voice say, "Cayman Islands." Too much of a coincidence. Had to be one of ours.

I put my finger to my lips, signaling Allison not to speak. She looked puzzled but complied. The voice had come from above us, over to the left. Behind another cluster of prickly shrubs. I walked closer, placing each sneakered foot carefully in the dim predawn light, trying not to dislodge rocks.

I could hear the murmur of two voices now, the woman's and a man's. They were speaking very quietly, but intently. Jody, I decided. And so, probably, Simon. Could one of them have dislodged the rocks that hit Allison?

"I never liked the idea," Jody said angrily, practically spitting out the words. "I never thought he'd play square with you. I told you. I told you that . . ."

"The most loathsome words between two people," said Simon furiously. "I told you, I told you," he mimicked. "You didn't tell me about your former lover's tax haven of choice, though, did you? Or how he was socking away my money as well as his in-laws' drug money?"

"What do you mean, your money? You have no money. It was my money . . . mine."

The venom between Simon and Jody Neel was ugly but edifying. I crept closer. Maybe I'd get the answers to all my remaining questions about Alan's death now.

"Is that you, Simon lamb? Jody? We're finally here," Allison sang out. I glared at her. She shrugged her shoulders and continued climbing. Why did she do that? I was so angry I couldn't follow her for several minutes. Admittedly, she'd known them for years and me for only a week. But I'd been so close to getting answers.

Allison must know of Simon's involvement in Alan's death, I thought. She'd intimated as much to me on a couple of occasions. So she was protecting him just now. Didn't want me to hear too much. What would I have heard?

The voices had stopped, then I could hear Jody greeting Allison. They had reached a kind of plateau, I could see, where a wide rock ledge reached out over the edge of the mountain like a giant's seat. Simon, Jody, and Allison were sitting on the ledge, drinking water, seemingly as relaxed as if they were at a café. Tom was sitting at their feet, eating a banana. He greeted me pleasantly enough, but with a definite reserve.

"There you are," Allison hailed me. "Come pull up a seat."

The Neels looked less than thrilled to have me join them, but Jody scooted closer to Simon to give me room on the ledge.

"Where's Phoebe?" I asked.

"Who knows? She might be keeping Cindy company at the back of the pack." Allison seemed unconcerned.

"Isn't that incredible?" asked Tom, pointing over my shoulder. "I never tire of it."

I twisted around on the rock ledge to see where he was looking. The narrowest sliver of pink was edging up from behind the peaks above us. With the burgeoning dawn came exquisitely sweet birdsong. My eyes filled with tears.

I stood to watch the sunrise and was now aware that the others too were standing on the broad ledge stretching, unselfconsciously doing the first postures of the yoga sun salutation. As I watched them, touched by the solemnity of the moment, I stepped up to the ledge and imitated their movements, holding my hands together in a prayer position, then reaching first way high above my head with my hands still together, lifting up out of my spine and curving slightly backward, then curving down to the ground, one vertebra at a time. After two such "salutes," the others glided into a slow, graceful lunge. I lunged not so gracefully, promptly losing my balance and landing on my rear. I decided to sit the rest out.

I sat down on the ground beneath the ledge and did some simpler leg stretches, then watched the others move as if effortlessly from one yoga posture to the next. I recognized the poses—there was the sphinx, the cobra, the cat, and (my least favorite) downward dog—but I wasn't tempted to join in. Climbing this high on Mount Cuchuma was accomplishment enough. After about ten minutes, I got restless and began to walk around the sentinel-like boulders at the crest of the mountain. On one side was a small signpost reading "Western slope. 3 mi. descent."

"Tempted to leave us all behind?" asked Tom.

I hadn't heard him come up beside me.

"I'd probably make a wrong turn."

"I don't think you could. It's all downhill from here."

"Ah, but it's where you end up that matters," said Allison, joining us. She was dabbing her damp forehead and neck with a small towel.

I started to laugh. "Too many subtle double entendres for me."

Tom rested his hand on my shoulder and smiled at me, then started off on the path down the mountain. Allison watched him for a moment, then walked back to the ledge, where she pulled a bottle of water out of her backpack.

Simon and Jody brushed past me without comment, but then Simon paused and walked back to me. Standing so close that I could see the pores in his movie star face, so close as to be menacing, he said with quiet intensity, "Leave it alone. We're all going away. That Mexican inspector may have suspicions but he doesn't have solid evidence. It's all circumstantial. He'll have to let us go. You let it go too, Nora. It would be wise." He held my eyes for a moment, then he turned, and he and Jody followed Tom down the path. I had to remind myself to breathe.

"Want any more water?" Allison called out to me cheerfully. I shook my head, not trusting myself to speak, and walked back to the ledge for my fanny pack. As I buckled it on, I glanced at Allison's backpack, lying on the edge of the rock. It was a lightweight canvas model, stuffed to capacity.

"Travel light, do you?" I asked, trying for humor. She smiled as she rearranged her possessions to make room for the bottle of water.

"What's that?" I asked, pointing at what appeared to be black fur in the open backpack. I reached out to touch it, but Allison grasped my hand. I realized it was a wig. I looked up at her, startled. She looked back at me silently. I felt sick.

"It was you. It was you, wasn't it?" I asked, looking up at the lovely, elegant woman I'd so admired. I shook off her hand. "Of course. Alan invested the money with you."

"Damn you, Nora. I told you, everyone told you, to let it alone."

"What a fool I've been." Allison must have heard the pain in my voice, because she winced. "Did every one know but me? I was so blind. You even told me you were working on your next million."

"I was almost there, too. I knew the Cerillos would demand an accounting someday, and I'd planned to get out at three million dollars."

I continued to stare at Allison. Her tracksuit was impeccably neat. Her hair was sleek, back from her face in a tidy golden braid. Her skin glistened from a light sheen of sweat and sunscreen. She was so beautiful. So funny and smart and interesting. My only real friend here.

She leaned over me and gripped my shoulders. I froze. She wouldn't, would she? We were completely alone here. The "posse" was long out of hearing range. We'd started climbing so late, there didn't appear to be anyone behind us. And now that the sun was beginning to rise like a fireball, I could see Allison's ice-blue glare all too clearly. For the first time, through my tears, I saw her clearly. I was consumed with rage, trembling, heedless of any possible danger to myself.

I shoved her, forcing her to release me. She stumbled, then grabbed my hand.

"You have to give me a break, Nora."

"The hell I do. Why do I owe you a break?"

"Because we're friends. I care about you. And you care about me."

"I did care about you. And that's why I'm so damned angry. You're a murderer!"

"It was an accident. We had an argument about the investments, and he tried to grab my backpack. I'd told him I had documents with me. It was an accident, I promise you. He fell."

"But you left him there. All night. And what about CeCe? You had to have planned her death. You're a murderer! And you tried to kill me. You followed me after our loving, intimate little talk the other night, and threw me down. You tried to suffocate me . . ."

"No, Nora, no. They were just warnings. If I'd wanted to really kill you, I could have. I just wanted to stop you from putting your nose where it didn't belong. You were like a hound dog!"

"Obviously not a good one; I never suspected you. Never. I trusted you. I won't make that mistake again."

I grabbed for Allison's backpack. What else was in there?

She pulled the bag away from me and swung it against my side. I almost fell, then pushed back at her. I slapped her, then really got into it and hit her again and again. I felt almost out of control, scratching at her face, yanking her braid, yelling, "Murderer, murderer." At first she hardly reacted, looking unbelieving. Then she hit me back.

I couldn't believe this. I'd never been physical, not even as a kid. No one had ever hit me before, and I certainly hadn't hit anyone else. Now we were locked in a maniacal embrace, shaking each other, pushing, kicking, slapping. I could feel blood dripping down my chin from my nose. I didn't even stop to wipe it away. Allison was stronger than I, but I was in such a rage I felt all-powerful.

All the while I was screaming at Allison, calling her a killer, a betrayer, accusing her of being a thief, a cheat, she didn't say a word. But when I taunted her that she was trash, that she was a money-hungry slut, she snarled at me, slapped me hard, and pushed me over onto the rocky ledge.

I fell on my hip and felt a muscle in my leg pull. I tried to relieve the pressure on the muscle by twisting away from my hip, then screamed, not realizing until then that I was sliding over the edge of the rocky ledge. There was nothing to grab on to. The sun had fully risen; the ranch below, very far below, was in sharp relief. I hung onto the ledge with my fingers, afraid to breathe, knowing I didn't have the strength to pull myself back up. I thought about Max. He'd never know how much I loved him.

"Allison," I cried.

It seemed like a month before I felt her grab my jacket and pull me back onto the ledge.

I lay there trembling, trying to steady my breathing, for long moments. Everything hurt: my leg, my hip, my nose. My soul. I looked up at Allison. Not so neat and cool any longer. She didn't take her eyes away from me. Nor did she look too happy about having saved my life. We both tried to control our breathing.

"I just need for you to climb down to the bottom of the mountain, slowly," she said finally. "To buy me some time before they realize I've gone missing. I'd planned this pretty carefully but didn't take you into account."

She was trembling but was almost unnaturally calm. I didn't say anything but watched her as she washed her face with her towel and the water in her backpack. She wound her braid up around her head and pinned it in place, then set the short, curly dark wig over it. She pulled a makeup kit out of the backpack, checked how the wig looked in a mirror, and began to apply fresh makeup, bolder and darker than her usual style. She put on thick silver hoop earrings and carefully inserted dark contact lenses. I watched, mesmerized, still breathing hard.

She was facing me, away from the path up the mountain. I could see, over her shoulder several hundred feet below, that there were two men climbing with steady difficulty up the mountain path. They were wearing warm-up suits and leather dress shoes, and they slipped on the rocks from time to time. I was almost sure I'd seen them in the municipal police headquarters the night before. I looked back at Allison. I said nothing.

Allison slipped on her backpack and looked at me. Neither of us spoke. She touched my shoulder, and when I shrugged off her hand, smiled sadly. She moved away from me and began walking quickly and surely down the northern slope of the mountain. She must have arranged for a car, I thought apathetically. I sat for a long time until I noticed the men approaching the ledge. I rose and with considerable discomfort started down the western slope of the mountain. Slowly.

ABOUT THE AUTHOR

Helen Barer, a native of New York City, divides her time between there and Water Mill, New York. She spent many years as a writer of nonfiction material, ranging from cookbooks to television documentaries. She is presently writing her next Nora Franke mystery.

Barer, Helen.
Fitness kills /